DOWNHILL CHALLENGE

STEPHEN D. SMITH with LISE CALDWELL

Standard
PUBLISHING
Bringing The Word to Life™

Cincinnati, Ohio

From Stephen

For Natalie and Carissa, for feedback on this story.
For all the readers of this book who like to go against
the flow and be yourselves.

From Lise

For Debbie and Dave, who taught me how to ski.

Text © 2006 Stephen Smith and Lise Caldwell. © 2006 Standard Publishing, Cincinnati,
Ohio. A division of Standex International Corporation. All rights reserved. Printed in the
United States of America. Project editors: Greg Holder, Lynn Lusby Pratt. Cover and
interior design: Rule29.

ISBN 0-7847-1735-4

12 11 10 09 08 07 06   9 8 7 6 5 4 3 2 1

Library of Congress Cataloging-in-Publication Data

Smith, Stephen D. (Stephen Dodd), 1961-
  Downhill challenge / Stephen D. Smith with Lise Caldwell.
      p. cm.
  Summary: Eighth-grader Beth asks God for guidance after she neglects her best
friend and withdraws from competitive snowboarding to become the girlfriend of a
popular classmate.
  ISBN 0-7847-1735-4 (pbk.)
  [1. Snowboarding--Fiction. 2. Popularity--Fiction. 3. Friendship--Fiction. 4. Christian life--
Fiction. 5. Wisconsin--Fiction.] I. Caldwell, Lise, 1974- II. Title.

PZ7.S659382Do 2006
[Fic]--dc22

2005031363

CHAPTER:01

The warm sun beamed down on Beth's upturned face. When she closed her eyes, she could almost imagine she was a little girl again, making clover-flower chains with her big sister Brooke down in the valley as the last of the snow melted higher up on Devil's Head Mountain.

But it wasn't spring, and Beth Summers wasn't a little girl anymore. Beth shielded her eyes from the snow glare, until she remembered that her sunglasses were on top of her head. Pulling them down over her eyes, she resented her forgetfulness. Beth always forgot stupid things when she was nervous. And being around her dad always made her nervous.

She adjusted her grip on the digital video camera she was holding. The brightness of the sun made it difficult to see the images on the LCD screen, with or without her sunglasses. But Dad always said mistakes were unacceptable. There were no second chances.

Beth bit her lip. How could she possibly shoot decent footage with this kind of glare and with the crowd of avid ski enthusiasts jostling her for position?

The sound of the gunshot from the top of the slope signaled the beginning of her sister Brooke's third downhill run of the day. Beth strained to hold the camera steady to capture the instant Brooke rounded the bend. Their mother, bundled in a heavy down coat, stood next to her, muttering something under her breath.

Brooke Summers was the best skier of the race today, but you couldn't tell it by the nervous look on her mother's face. Beth's only concern was to capture Brooke's run to her father's satisfaction, so that he could later pick apart every weakness in Brooke's performance.

Her father stood a few steps away. It looked like his eyes were closed, but Beth knew he was just squinting, not from the sun, but from the mental focus of the race. He gripped a stopwatch tightly in his hand. He never trusted the electronic sensors on the slopes and always tracked Brooke's speed himself. His knees were slightly bent as if he, not his oldest daughter, were the one competing.

A moment later, Brooke's slender figure zoomed into the LCD frame. Beth didn't dare look at the actual slope, but she did manage to keep Brooke's image on-screen as she followed the progress of the remainder of the run. It was no easy task, considering Brooke rocketed off a jump, went airborne, and executed a stunning 450-degree turn, and then skied down *in reverse* before completing another 450-degree turn, which sent her cruising toward the finish line facing forward and at top speed.

Beth hoped her dad was satisfied. At least she hadn't forgotten to take off the lens cap as she had at the Alpine Valley Juniors Invitational last month.

Beth watched Brooke spray snow as she skied to a stop and removed her goggles. The crowd applauded wildly. As a local girl, Brooke Summers was always a crowd favorite. Beth continued filming, unwilling to stop until her dad had given her the OK.

Beth watched her sister on the little screen. She looked more like a swimsuit model than a skier. Her face was tan from all her time on the slopes, and her hair was bleached golden blond by the sun. She was one of those people whose smile made you smile. Beth's mind swirled with a combination of love, admiration, and envy. It just wasn't fair that her sister was so perfect.

Beth turned off the camera as soon as Brooke's image was blocked by her mother, father, and Brooke's boyfriend Ty, who taught skiing and snowboarding at Devil's Head.

For a moment, Beth imagined *she* was the one surrounded by friends and family, coming off a winning run. The only difference would be she wouldn't have skis and poles. She'd land with her snowboard after a twisting jump. Oh, and her father wouldn't be there.

Her father was Brooke's coach, mentor, trainer, and agent. He poured his life into preparing her for success on the slopes—on skis. When Beth was younger she'd skied too, and occasionally got some help from her dad, usually when Brooke had homework. But most of her training had come naturally. As year-round residents of Devil's Head, the Summers family lived on the slopes. Their house was just a mile from the town ski resort, and Beth had skied every day as a child. She had idolized her older sister Brooke.

But two winters ago, she'd snowboarded for the first time when her best friend Reed had loaned her his board. She didn't think she'd like it, but her love for the sport was instant.

Her father, however, was less enthusiastic. He viewed snowboarding as the domain of "hoodlums and slackers." She'd practiced in secret, whenever she could borrow a board, until she was really good. Brooke and her mom encouraged her, but that didn't remove the sting of her father's disapproval.

Beth's daydream was interrupted by the voice of the announcer:

"Ladies and gentlemen, the judges' final scores are in for the combined downhill-slalom event. In third place is Jess Winston with a time of 9.825 minutes. In second place is Rachel Crowe at 8.992 minutes." After a pause, the announcer, with his voice raised, shouted, "And today's champion is a Devil's Head native—nineteen-year-old Brooke Summers, with a record-tying time of 8.125 minutes. Congratulations, champions!"

Beth ran through the snow to congratulate her sister. Brooke threw her arms around her.

"Thanks for being here!" Brooke said. "Knowing you're here always makes me push even harder."

Beth smiled and hugged Brooke back. "You were terrific, Brooke. That second jump was one of your best yet."

Brooke started to say thanks when her father interrupted. "It was good, Brooke, but you really should have held your poles up like torches during the spins."

"Oh, please, Gary," Beth's mom said. "She was wonderful. She won, didn't she?"

"Sure, but do you think this is the caliber of competition she'll have at the Olympic trials?"

Brooke looked at Beth and rolled her eyes as their parents moved away, continuing to argue. Brooke put her arm around her little sister.

"Are you joining us tonight for pizza, or do you and your friends have a movie planned?" Brooke asked.

"I wouldn't miss your victory party for anything!" Beth said.

"Great! I need to head back to school late tonight. I'm on the worship team at campus fellowship in the morning."

"Come on, Jake," the voice called through the handheld walkie-talkie. "Show us what you've got!"

Jake Bahlman stood at the top of the Devil's Playground run, watching another boarder out of the corner of his eye. Then he bent his knees and bounced on them lightly, just as he'd seen the other guy do. Although Devil's Playground was considered one of the easier slopes—just a novice run—it was more than enough for Jake to handle. He wondered if he'd exaggerated his skills when he convinced some of the other eighth-grade guys to come and watch him board. He was comforted slightly by the knowledge that he was at least a better boarder than any of them were.

"I'm going for it," Jake called out to his friend Ian Carter. "Start the camera."

"I already did," Ian shouted from the bottom of the slope. Jake pushed off, and as he descended, he zoomed back and forth across the slope. He hoped this looked impressive, but in reality it was only a technique to keep his speed under control.

As he approached the point where the slope split into two paths, Jake mustered enough courage to take the left run, which led to a small jump.

"It'll make for fantastic footage," his friend Ian had said earlier.

Jake just hoped his jump wouldn't make the local papers—as the first fatality of the season.

With a burst of adrenaline, Jake straightened himself up and leaned into the board to build speed. The wind rushed past him, blowing bitterly on his face. As he rocketed over the jump, he remembered Ian's request for a spin. In a split-second decision, Jake attempted a 360-degree turn and was almost completely turned around when his board made contact with the powdery snow. He barely kept himself from falling. It wasn't graceful, but he wasn't maimed either. Confidently, he boarded down the last leg of the slope to where his friends awaited his arrival.

"You got six feet of air that time," Scottie Granger said.

"So, how was it? Not too terrible?" Jake sounded more humble than he felt.

"It was good," Ian replied.

"Good?" said Scottie. "It was stinkin' fantastic! We should come here more often."

"How about Monday after school?" Jake asked. "I bet I could get Reed Nagle to come with us."

"That weirdo?" Scottie asked.

"That weirdo has the best snowboard at school," Jake replied, "and I want to try it out."

While Beth had been relegated to the opposite end of the long wooden table at Rosetta's Stone Oven Pizza, Brooke sat at the head, with Dad sitting on her left and Ty to her right. Even Ty's parents and eight-year-old twin brothers sat closer to Brooke than she.

"I'm sorry," Brooke mouthed, but it didn't compensate for having to put up with the bratty twins.

That's why Brooke was so eager to have me here, Beth thought, *so I could babysit the demon brothers.*

Beth knew she wasn't being fair to Brooke, but by the third time one of the twins—Brock or Blake . . . she never could tell which—had knocked her water glass off the table, she wasn't that interested in being fair.

Just as she was pondering how long the jail term would be for a double homicide, Reed Nagle and his family walked through the door.

Beth couldn't believe she'd forgotten that the Nagles came to Rosetta's practically every Friday night. The Nagles were big on tradition—obsessed,

Beth sometimes thought. They seemed to have rituals for all of their family times: Christmas, Easter, St. Patrick's Day, and the second Tuesday of months that started with the letter *J*. In her more honest moments, Beth thought it was cool. After all, the Nagles were really close and had a blast together. Actually, Beth had a blast *with* them, even when she had to participate in the Nagle Semiannual Backwards Bowling Night.

Beth quickly locked eyes with Reed. "Help!" Beth mouthed. Reed nodded.

A question from Ty's father brought Beth's attention back to the party. "So, Beth," he asked, "do you plan to follow in your sister's footsteps?"

Beth hesitated. She wasn't in the mood to spark a debate on the merits of snowboarding. Before she could answer, her father interrupted.

"She has a great deal of potential, George," Beth's dad said. "But she can't seem to get it through her head that it takes practice and dedication. She's more concerned with hanging out with her little friends and their snowboards."

"Daddy, that's not fair," Brooke whispered. The table grew uncomfortably quiet.

"So when's that new lift going to be up and running, Ty?" Beth's mom asked, trying to change the subject.

At that moment, Reed appeared at Beth's side.

"Good thing you're here," Beth whispered. "I was about to commit a crime."

"Felony or misdemeanor?" Reed asked.

"That depends," Beth replied, "on whether I could make an attack on two eight-year-old brats look like self-defense."

Reed grinned and then cleared his throat. "Excuse me, Mr. and Mrs. Summers. Would it be OK if Beth came and sat with my family for a while?"

Mr. Summers hesitated, so Reed added, "Mom and Dad are anxious to hear Beth's account of Brooke's victory today." Beth stepped on his foot as he said it, but it worked.

"Suit yourself," Beth's dad replied. "You could watch the footage if Beth hadn't jiggled the camera so much. Wouldn't want you to lose your pizza."

Beth stifled a growl and quickly escaped from the table.

"I owe you one," Beth whispered.

"You've been saying that since I took the blame for that chocolate milk fiasco in kindergarten. Not a pretty scene."

"How was I supposed to know that even *chocolate* milk would trigger lactose intolerance?" Beth replied.

"Just letting you know I'm keeping a tab," Reed said with a grin.

Reed's family eagerly made a place for Beth at their table. "What'll it be, Summers?" Mr. Nagle asked.

"Prosciutto and pineapple pizza, please," she said.

"Very good. I think I'll have the same," he replied.

Reed leaned over and whispered, "You're just showing off because you can say *prosciutto*."

"Hey," she said, "if you've got it, flaunt it."

Reed rolled his eyes and laughed. Beth glanced back at the table where her family sat. Her father was lecturing on something—probably the finer points of aerial acrobatics. Beth felt like she'd escaped from a dungeon.

Beth hoped the Nagles didn't think she was a pig for wanting another pizza, but Brock and Blake had kept her so busy she hadn't eaten a bite of her own.

Mr. Nagle ordered for them, managing to pronounce *prosciutto* with just a little coaching from the waitress, and the Nagles asked Beth about Brooke's competition that day. Usually it irritated her when people asked her about Brooke, but she knew the Nagles cared about both girls. So Beth cheerfully told them about Brooke's victory at Devil's Head.

The pizzas arrived. Beth had learned after many meals with the Nagles that nobody ate until they had thanked God for their food. This time, Reed said the blessing.

"Dear Heavenly Father, thank you for this delicious pizza and for the time we're spending together as a family. Thanks for Beth being here too. Help each of us to please you in everything that we do. In Jesus' name we pray. Amen."

During the prayer, Beth peeked at Reed a few times. It always seemed strange to her that he talked to God that way—like God was someone he knew and really cared about. Beth's parents prayed, usually only at church, but their prayers were memorized, not personal. Beth didn't know anyone besides the Nagle family who seemed to be really close to God, except maybe Brooke since she'd gone off to college. Beth wanted to understand it all and maybe even be a part of it, but she wasn't sure how.

While she devoured her pizza, Beth had a great time listening to Mr. Nagle's stories about growing up in Texas. Beth couldn't quite imagine any place so flat and hot. Mr. Nagle had never even seen snow until he came to Wisconsin for college.

"I sat outside all night long the first snow of my freshman year," he told them. "No coat, no hat, nothing but a sweatshirt Mom had gotten me at the campus bookstore. I couldn't stop watching that beautiful snow fall down. It made the world look so peaceful. So pure. I had just become a Christian, and I thought the snow was the best picture of God's grace that I'd ever seen. Right then I promised myself that I'd always live someplace where it snowed."

All too soon, Beth's dad waved at her from across the restaurant. Then he pointed to his watch. *Time to go,* she thought. She thanked the Nagles and excused herself. Reed walked her to the door.

"See you later, mashed potater," Beth said, using the same good-bye they'd used since they were eight.

"After while, onion pile," he replied.

That night, as Beth snuggled deeper under the covers, she heard hushed but angry voices coming from her parents' bedroom. *Another fight,* she thought. *And it's probably about me.* She knew her mom stood up for her, but it never seemed to make a difference. Nothing Beth did—nothing *any* of them did—was ever good enough for her father.

Beth thought about Reed's prayer. He'd called God his "Father." Why? Could God be a father to her too? She sure wished she could trade hers in for a less critical one.

As she drifted off to sleep, she muttered, "God, why can't my dad be more like you?"

CHAPTER:02

After school on Monday, Reed headed for his locker and spotted Jake standing in front of it. It was too late to avoid him. Jake and Reed had been in school together since they were little kids, and even played on the same baseball team last summer, but Jake wasn't exactly a friend.

"What's up, Jake?" Reed asked. He dialed the combination on his locker, figuring the quicker he got this over with, the better.

"I was thinking maybe you should come snowboarding with us after school today."

"Why?" Reed asked.

"Because we haven't hung around since last summer. I thought it would be cool."

Reed was curious, but not fooled for a minute. Jake the jock considered him a geek.

"Sure," Reed said slowly. "Why not?"

"Scott, Ian, and Nick are coming too," Jake

said. "My mom will pick you up. How about four o'clock?"

"Fine," Reed said. He'd have to wait until after school to solve the mystery of why Jake had invited him.

Beth opened the back door and entered her house through the mudroom. She took off her boots and hung up her coat as her sister greeted her at the kitchen doorway.

"Hey, sis," Brooke said, "got any plans for this afternoon?"

Beth looked at her sister curiously.

"Because if you don't," Brooke teased as Beth noticed her hands behind her back, "I think I might have a good idea!"

Brooke pulled out a pink snowboard decorated with white flowers. The bottom of the board had a pink oval on it about the size of her foot. Inside the oval were the words *Snow Bunny*.

"Happy early birthday, sis!" Brooke said with an excited smile on her face.

"But my birthday is in June!" Beth said with a puzzled look on her face.

"Don't you like it?" Brooke replied, sounding disappointed.

"No!" Beth said. "I mean yes! Are you kidding? I love it! I just don't get it."

"Since I'm in college on a scholarship, I used some of my college fund. I just wanted to buy my little sister a present to show her how much I love her!"

Beth hugged Brooke tightly. Then she grabbed the board and examined it. The bindings were already attached.

"So?" Brooke asked.

"So . . . what?" Beth asked back.

"So . . . let's go try it out!"

Within fifteen minutes, Beth was dressed and ready for the slopes. They rode together in Brooke's bright yellow Jeep that had a fabulous stereo system, and Brooke cranked up the volume. Beth had never heard the song before. The lead singer was a girl with a gritty, gutsy voice. At first Beth thought it was a love song, but soon she realized the girl was singing about Jesus.

"Who is that anyway?" Beth asked.

Brooke's face broke out in a goofy, embarrassed grin. "It's me!"

"What?"

"Well, me and the rest of the praise band from church. We cut a CD in a basement studio a few weeks ago. Do you like it?"

Beth was stunned. She never even knew her sister could sing. There wasn't much chance to join a choir when you had to ski four hours a day.

"It's great!" Beth said. "I'm just surprised, that's all."

"I guess I'm full of surprises today then," Brooke replied.

"Thanks for the board," Beth said. "I really do love it."

"You deserve to have one of your own. But I didn't know when Daddy would break down and get you one. So I figured that was my job."

At the mention of their dad, Beth grew quiet.

"Beth," Brooke said, "Daddy hurt your feelings last night. I saw it on your face. I know you think he's hard on you, but believe it or not, he's even like that to me when we're practicing. I've just learned to take it. He doesn't mean to be so critical. He loves you just as much as he loves me—really."

"I think if I just told him I was done with snowboarding, things would be better," Beth said.

"But that's not who you are, Beth," Brooke said.

"Maybe not, Brooke," Beth replied, "but I don't know how much more of it I can take."

"I know, sweetie," Brooke said.

"I mean," Beth went on, "snowboarding is an Olympic sport too! It's basically skiing on one big ski."

"Dad will get used to it, eventually," Brooke said.

"I'm not going to worry about it right now," Beth said. "Let's just break in this new board!"

"That's my girl!" Brooke said. She smiled and ruffled Beth's hair.

The snow was fresh that afternoon. Jake and Reed rode the red metal chairlift together. Reed looked out over the mountain at the evergreen trees blanketed with a layer of powdery snow.

Dad's right, Reed thought. *The snow does make everything beautiful.*

Scottie and Nick rode the lift behind them. When they were kids, Reed had enjoyed hanging out with Scott and Nick. They'd played kickball together on summer evenings at the end of Nick's cul-de-sac. But since middle school, they'd become Jake Bahlman followers and didn't talk to Reed much anymore—unless Jake spoke to him first.

Ian stood at the bottom of the slope with the video camera ready to film. Ian was a good guy. Reed often ran into him at Atomic Comics. He didn't ski much and never boarded, but he loved to film it all. One of the music videos he made had already won some local awards. Reed figured Ian was here at Jake's invitation as well.

When the boys reached the top, Jake said, trying to sound casual, "Hey, mind if we trade boards on the first run?"

Now it was all clear to Reed. *He just wanted to use my new board.* Reed didn't mind loaning it out, but he didn't like that Jake was using him.

"Sure," Reed said. "I just waxed it yesterday."

Jake's eyes widened slightly, but he didn't say anything. Reed got the feeling that a freshly waxed board wasn't exactly what Jake was up for.

Even so, Reed was surprised at the speed Jake picked up at the top of the run. It took a few seconds for him to gain some control of the board and begin zigzagging down the slope to slow himself down. Reed and the other guys followed in intervals.

Brooke and Beth arrived at the top of Devil's Alley, a difficult ski slope with some sweet jumps. Beth had mastered the beginner and intermediate runs on skis by the time she was ten. Even this slope didn't frighten her on skis. But now, it was time to try it on a board—a *new* board—and she was nervous. Balancing on two skis was a lot easier than balancing on one board. Brooke encouraged her.

"You start down," Brooke said, "and I'll ski down after you. We'll meet up at the bottom of the slope."

Beth stood on her new board and wriggled her feet in her boots to make sure she was comfortable. Putting all of her weight on her heels, she clicked her boots into the bindings. She stood at the crest of the mountain looking down the slope and then back at her sister. Brooke nodded, and Beth dropped into the slope. The force of her jump helped her build speed quickly, and before she knew it, she was pursuing the vacant trail downhill, with Brooke ten seconds behind her.

Beth approached the sign for a platform jump and stayed to the left, daring herself to take on the jump. She squatted down and pushed her upper body forward, sailing over the snow-covered wooden platform and hurtling ten feet into the air. Beth had never done this before. Now she knew what it was to fly!

Jake had gotten control of Reed's board by the time he reached the bottom of the slope. He glided past Ian, who was manning the camera, and kept going until his speed slowly decreased. He came to a stop at the foot of the Devil's Alley run just as Beth sped past. She kicked her board up into a fast stop, spraying Jake with snow. Beth lifted her goggles, and Jake did the same. Reed, Nick, and Scott arrived right behind, while Brooke skied over from the right.

"Hey, Beth," Jake said, "I didn't know you boarded."

I didn't know you knew my name! Beth thought. Jake Bahlman was the most popular boy at school and generally made her feel invisible.

"Hey, Jake," Beth replied. "Yeah, I love to snowboard."

"Hi, Beth," Reed called as he approached. "What're you doing here?"

Beth explained that she and Brooke had come to try out her new board.

"Brooke? Brooke Summers? She's your sister?" Jake asked in surprise.

"Unless she was kidnapped by aliens and replaced with a cyborg," Beth replied.

Beth realized what she'd done when Reed snorted. She'd made fun of Jake Bahlman. Quickly, she tried to recover.

"I mean, yes, she is," Beth said. "Would you like to meet her?"

Jake, Nick, and Scott were all eager to be introduced to the skiing sensation too. Ian already had the camera rolling again.

"Miss Summers," Jake said, "it really is a pleasure to meet you. Can I have your autograph?"

Beth was certain she heard Reed whisper, "Fanboy," but she ignored him.

"Sure," Beth's sister said.

"Hey, Ian!" Jake called. "Come take my picture with Brooke Summers."

Jake got into position as Ian took out his digital camera. Reed shook his head in disgust, but Beth was used to Brooke drawing crowds lately.

When the guys had gotten their autographs and pictures taken, Brooke suggested they go back to the top of the slope and do some runs together.

"Sure!" Jake said eagerly. He stood next to Brooke in the lift line, obviously hoping to ride up with her. Beth was a little irritated. After all, this was supposed to be a sister day.

But Brooke didn't let her down. "Come on, Beth," she said. "This chair is for girls only. See you guys at the top."

When they all got off the lift, Brooke began to quiz the guys about their skills and their interest in snowboarding as a competitive sport.

"Whoa," Nick said, "we're just along for the ride. If you're looking for a serious boarder, Jake's your man."

Jake looked pleased, but wondered if he could live up to his reputation. After all, this was Brooke Summers, Olympic hopeful.

"OK then, Jake," she said. "Show us what you've got."

Brooke borrowed Beth's new board and followed Jake and Scott down the run. Beth waited with Reed at the top, along with Ian.

"Aren't you going too?" Beth asked Reed.

"Not with Jake's board."

"Where's yours?" she asked.

"Jake borrowed it," he said. Beth thought it was strange that Reed had loaned Jake his board. Reed had never thought much of Jake.

"Not skiing today, Ian?" Reed asked.

"I prefer filming to plowing my head into a tree," Ian said. "I'll ride the lift down."

"Maybe you can work for ESPN someday," Reed said. "They'd probably love a guy like you." Ian grinned.

Just like Reed to say the right thing, Beth thought.

"Why don't I ride down with you?" Reed suggested. "Then you can set up and film Beth's run. She's awesome."

"Plus she's a whole lot prettier than Jake," Ian added.

Beth knew they were just joking around. No one ever called Beth pretty. "You must be thinking of Brooke," she said.

"The camera doesn't lie!" Ian said. "Let's go, Reed."

Beth waited alone at the top for them ride back down. She saw Jake and Brooke returning on the chairlift. They both waved.

"Where are Ian and Reed?" Jake yelled.

Beth pointed to the bottom of slope. "Ian is going to film me jumping the platform," Beth yelled.

"You jump the Devil's Alley platform?" Jake said in surprise, skiing off the lift.

"She just did it for the first time and was awesome," Brooke told him.

"Great," Jake said, but he didn't sound convinced. "Let's do the run together."

"That's cool," Beth said, holding Jake's snowboard.

She handed it to him, and he handed Reed's to Brooke. The three prepared for their next run as Nick and Scott approached on the lift.

"Jake," Brooke instructed, "pull back with me and let Beth take the lead."

Launching herself over the edge and into the run, Beth eased herself into the slope, swooping back and forth from one evergreen-lined side to the other. She came out of a slight curve and into a straightaway that led down to the platform. She couldn't see Reed or Ian, but as she built up speed, she hoped they were both smart enough not to be set up twenty feet under the ramp, directly in her path.

Beth shot across the platform and out over the slope. As she did, she jerked her body into a spin and was surprised that she completed a 360-degree turnaround with no difficulty. She had plenty of time to get her bearings before making contact with the snow. As she sped down, she heard loud applause from Reed and Ian. She turned slightly to see that they had set up across from the jump.

Beth looked back just in time to see Jake approach the platform and take the jump. She could see the fear on his face. She watched as Jake leaned into his board, and as he hit the surface, his weight drove the front of the board into the snow. Wipe out!

Beth, Ian, Reed, and Brooke rushed to where Jake lay stunned in the snow.

"That was awesome," Ian said.

"You have no idea!" Jake shouted as Reed grabbed his hand and pulled him to his feet. "I've never felt anything like that!"

"Good try," Brooke said. "It'll be easier next time."

"Beth, I got some awesome footage of you coming off the platform," Ian said excitedly. "You too, Jake."

"You guys looked really good out there," Reed added.

"Thanks," Jake said, turning to Beth. "Man, you're awesome, Beth. You should come here with us more often. We come almost every day after school."

"Thanks," Beth said. "It would be nice to get out here more often."

"My mom could pick you up on the way," Jake added. "The only reason we have five today is because Reed came."

"Oh," Beth said. She wondered why Reed wouldn't be coming anymore. Without him, this wouldn't have been half as fun. But she couldn't turn down the chance to get on her new board some more. She glanced at Brooke, who looked irritated.

"Reed," Brook said, "why don't we give you a ride home? It's on our way."

Beth was surprised by how relieved Reed looked. "That'd be great. That is," he said, turning to Jake, "if that's OK with you and your mom."

"I don't care what you do, Nagle," Jake said. "But thanks for bringing your board. See you soon, Summers," he said, holding Beth's gaze until she looked down in embarrassment.

Nick, Jake, Scott, and Ian headed out to wait for Mrs. Bahlman. Reed, Beth, and Brooke did one more run, but Reed had retreated into himself.

CHAPTER:03

Beth's first period class was World Civ. Her teacher, Mrs. Grafton, was big on group projects—really big. Beth, on the other hand, was not such a fan. She liked to work on her own. Maybe that was why she was a snowboarder. Whenever she was in a group, it seemed like she was always the one doing twice as much work as anyone else.

So on Tuesday when Mrs. Grafton announced that she was dividing up the class into groups of three to do a project on society in the Middle Ages, Beth groaned. But her irritation was nothing compared to her misery when she heard with whom she was grouped—Kimberly "Kimmy" Carmichael and Michelle Honeycutt. Kimmy and Michelle were best friends. Half their time, as far as Beth could tell, was spent fighting over boys, and the other half, shopping or talking about clothes.

Kimmy was blond and Michelle was a redhead,

but otherwise they looked, dressed, and acted the same. They never turned in homework, and how they scraped by from one grade to the next had been a mystery to Beth—until she found out Kimmy's dad was on the school board and Michelle's dad had made several large donations to the school library. Beth would be surprised if Kimmy or Michelle could even *find* the library.

Mrs. Grafton gave them the rest of class time to discuss their project. Beth gathered her books together and moved. She knew Kimmy and Michelle would never give up their prime seats by the window where they could watch the eighth-grade boys' gym class run laps in the snow around the soccer field.

Beth felt sick to her stomach as she got out her note-book. Neither of the other girls even looked at her.

"There's Jake Bahlman," Kimmy said. "Who's he going out with now?"

"Nobody," Michelle replied. "He just broke up with Kendra."

"Really? That's too bad," Kimmy said, but Beth didn't think she sounded at all sorry to hear the news. "I wonder if that's why he didn't come to El Diablo's yesterday."

"Actually, he was at the slopes yesterday after-noon," Beth told them.

They both turned and looked at her as if watching

the birth of an alien creature. "How do *you* know?" Michelle asked.

"Because we snowboarded together," Beth said.

Beth could almost hear the gears whirring in their heads. *Her?* she knew they were thinking. *With Jake?* This was new information, and new information was hard for Kimmy and Michelle to process.

Suddenly, Kimmy looked at Beth with a huge smile that showed almost all of her straight white teeth.

"So what do you think we should do for our project, Beth? I'm sure you have some fantastic ideas."

"Fantastic," echoed Michelle.

Beth spent the rest of class trying to explain the basics of chivalry and the feudal system, but without much success. Kimmy kept arguing that they were called the Dark Ages because of a massive lightbulb shortage, and Michelle couldn't understand that serfs were slaves and not surfers.

But when the bell rang, Kimmy surprised Beth by saying, "Why don't you sit with us at lunch today? We'd love to hear more about your snowboarding."

Beth hesitated, but agreed, and then wished she could take back her words. She knew Kimmy and Michelle were up to something.

Beth saw the look of surprise on Reed's face when she sat down with the two popular girls. She smiled and waved at him across the cafeteria, and he waved back.

Her lunch with K and M (as she thought of them) wasn't so bad really. They talked a lot about boys and clothes, and Beth got quite an education in both. And they asked her lots of questions about snowboarding. She wasn't kidding herself. She knew who would do all the work on the World Civ project—*and* she knew the girls had a hidden agenda.

"So," Kimmy asked, polishing off three grapes and a strawberry, "are you going together with Jake?"

"If you mean going together to the slopes again, then, yeah, I think we're going this afternoon."

Kimmy looked at Michelle, but made no comment. "Do you just go and watch him? I hear he's really good."

Again, Beth wasn't sure what to say. She didn't want to sound like she was bragging.

"Actually, I snowboard too." *And I'm much better than Jake*, she thought.

"Oh," said Michelle. "Is that why you dress like that?"

"Like what?" Beth asked. She wore a baggy sweater, blue jeans, and hiking boots practically every day.

Then she looked at Kimmy's pretty sweater, corduroy skirt, tights, and boots. Michelle had on trendy pants and a matching top, and her jewelry was perfect. They both wore eye shadow and lip gloss.

"Never mind, Beth," Kimmy said. "It's just that we never could have known what a cool girl you are by the way you dress."

Beth wasn't sure if she should say thank you or be insulted. Before she could think of an answer, the bell rang. The three of them cleared their trays and headed for their next classes.

Beth spent every afternoon that week at the slopes, perfecting her technique on the new board. She enjoyed hanging out with Nick, Scott, and Ian —and especially Jake. She wondered about what Kimmy had said and whether Jake liked her. But then she thought about the kind of girls Jake usually went for. They all had great clothes and perfect hair. No, Jake just liked snowboarding with her. That's all. For some reason, she felt a little disappointed.

When Beth's doorbell rang at eleven o'clock on Saturday morning, she knew who it was. For as long as she could remember, Reed had come to her house every Saturday. They used to watch cartoons and eat chocolate chip pancakes together. Now they usually just popped in a movie, but they still ate the chocolate chip pancakes.

Beth studied the clothes she had thrown all over her bed. She'd decided that Kimmy and Michelle might actually be onto something. Maybe it wasn't such a bad thing to wear pretty clothes and makeup.

Beth had borrowed a few of Brooke's outfits to try on. The girls were almost the same height, but Brooke was a little curvier. As Beth tried on each outfit, she turned to look at her profile, hoping to find something that wouldn't make her look like a little girl. So far, no luck.

She was just trying on the last outfit when her mother yelled up that Reed was downstairs. Beth frowned. She'd hoped to change back into her usual grubbies before he got there. No time for that now. She whipped open her door and ran down in one of Brooke's outfits.

"Going someplace?" Reed asked in surprise.

"No," she said, trying to hide her embarrassment. "Just trying on some of Brooke's clothes."

"You look really different dressed like that," he said.

Beth really wished he'd stop talking about her clothes. "Do I look that bad?" she asked.

Beth was surprised to see Reed's ears turn pink. "No, um . . . you don't look bad at all. Actually," he said, "I think I'll go see if your mom needs help with the pancakes." Reed turned on his heels and practically ran across the great room.

Beth wondered what was wrong with him anyway, but she was too hungry for pancakes to worry about it. She headed for the kitchen and found Reed pouring batter onto the hot griddle, while her mother poured orange juice.

"Morning, sweetie," her mom said.

"Morning." Beth walked up behind Reed and peered down at the griddle. "Make sure mine's done all the way through."

Beth's mother tucked a book under her arm and carried a glass of orange juice into the great room.

"So," Reed said, "I've hardly seen you this week. What's been going on?"

"I've gone snowboarding every afternoon this week—"

"With Jake?" Reed interrupted.

"And Scott and Nick," Beth said.

Reed studied the pancakes. "How's the 450-degree coming?" he asked.

"Fine, I guess," she said. "When I'm at the slopes with the guys, I end up helping them more than getting to practice my own stuff."

"Wow," Reed said sarcastically, "that sounds like fun."

Beth didn't get it. What was Reed's problem today? "Plus I've been hanging out with Kimmy and Michelle."

"Making progress on the Middle Ages?"

"Very little, actually," Beth said. "It's hard to make them focus." And truthfully, Beth had almost stopped trying.

"Great week you're having then," Reed said.

"What's your problem this morning?" Beth asked.

"It's just that you're at the slopes, but you're not practicing your moves, and you're spending tons of time with Kimmy and Michelle, but not finishing your project."

"So?" Beth asked.

"Seems to me you're losing your focus," Reed said. "I just don't want to see that happen."

"You sound just like my dad." Beth stood up. "What's wrong with me just hanging out with my friends?"

"Nothing," Reed said. "It's just that I thought *I* was your friend."

Beth plopped back down in her chair. "Of course you're my friend—my very best friend. I'm just making some new friends too, OK?"

"OK," Reed said. He handed Beth a stack of pancakes. "So, what're you doing tonight?"

"Jake and some people are going to El Diablo's," she said.

"By *some people* do you mean the regular crew of Jake followers?"

"I guess," she said, feeling irritated again. "You could come too, you know."

"No thanks," Reed said. "Remember, we changed Anime Club to Saturday night this week? We're watching *Sky Island*, volumes one and two."

"Oh, wow," Beth said. "I totally forgot. I'm sorry, but I already told Jake I could come."

They ate the remainder of their pancakes in silence. Beth hated this new distance between them, but was it bad to make new friends?

Reed looked at his watch. "I gotta go."

"Aren't we going to watch some TV?"

"Maybe some other time. See you Monday," he said, walking out. He stopped and turned. "Unless you want to come with me to youth group tomorrow night."

Beth wasn't sure if she was up for youth group with Reed this weekend. Things were just too weird between them right now.

"I'll let you know," she said.

"Fine," he said, leaving. "Bye."

Beth stared at her sticky plate. Why was Reed so annoyed with her? When her mom walked in the door a few minutes later, Beth was still sitting there.

"Where's Reed?" her mom asked.

"He left," Beth said. When she stood up, she could hear her mother's surprise.

"What are you wearing?" she asked.

Why was it such a big deal to everyone? "I was just trying on some of Brooke's old clothes. I wanted something new to wear to El Diablo's tonight."

Her mom studied her closely. "Are you wearing makeup too?"

Beth had forgotten that she'd put on some eye shadow and lip gloss. "Yeah, a little, I guess. Is that a problem?"

Her mom sighed. "No, it's OK with me. But your father will have a fit."

"*Mom!*" Beth said. "All the eighth-grade girls I know wear makeup."

"Calm down, sweetie," she said. "I'll talk to your dad. In the meantime, just don't let him see you like that."

Beth stomped upstairs to wash her face. What was the big deal anyway? As she scrubbed off the makeup, she decided she really did need to get going on the World Civ project and some other homework she'd gotten behind on that week. Watching TV with Reed would only have postponed the inevitable, and this way she'd have time to finish before snowboarding that afternoon.

She got so interested in reading about the First and Second Crusades that she didn't realize how late it was until Brooke knocked on her door and opened it. "Hey, that's one of my old outfits, isn't it?" Brooke said in surprise. "Is that what you're going to wear this afternoon?"

"Maybe," Beth said. "What do you think?"

"It looks like you slept in it," Brooke said. "Have you been wearing it all day?"

Beth nodded and looked down at the wrinkles—

something she hadn't paid much attention to before.

"I don't think you've got time to iron it, so let's pick out something else," Brooke said. Beth grinned, and they headed for Brooke's closet.

With Brooke's expert advice, Beth soon was dressed in a pink, fitted button-down shirt, a brown skirt, matching tights and shoes, and even a pink purse. Beth thought the pink purse was a little ridiculous, but Brooke insisted.

"There," Brooke said, standing back to admire her handiwork. "You look beautiful."

Beth just smiled. *I hope so,* she thought. She really wanted Jake to think so too.

Brooke dropped Beth off in front of the restaurant. "What time should I pick you up?" she asked.

"Don't worry about it," Beth said. "Jake's mom will give me a ride home."

"Great," Brooke said. "I'm going to head back to campus tonight. Have a great time. See you next weekend!"

Beth hated that Brooke wasn't home full-time anymore. On impulse, she hugged her sister and got out of Brooke's Jeep.

"Love you!" Brooke said and drove away.

El Diablo's was the hot spot in town. Situated just four blocks from Beth's house, it offered great burgers and ice cream treats, and according to a certificate framed on the wall above the cash register, the very best hot chocolate in all of Wisconsin.

The restaurant, housed in a hundred-year-old red brick building, was cozy. An enormous fireplace always crackled with flames. The owners, who had purchased the place in the 1980s, shopped antique shows and flea markets all over Wisconsin to find vintage booths and old tins. Overhead, a rack supported a collection of ice cream containers, syrup cans and jars, malt tins, and old tin signs from ice cream makers. Vintage photos of downtown Merrimac and the first chairlift on the slopes hung on the walls.

She stood uncertainly in the doorway until someone walking past bumped into her. It was Ian.

"Where are you going?" Beth asked.

"Anime night over at Reed's. Have fun." He spotted Beth's group. "They're all sitting over there," he said, pointing. "Bunch of vipers."

Beth headed in the direction Ian had pointed. Kimmy squealed, "Beth!"

Relieved to have found her friends, Beth slipped into the large booth next to Jake. Scott sat next to him, and Kimmy, Michelle, and Nick sat across from them.

Even though it was a large booth, Jake hadn't made much room for her on the end. She found herself sitting closer to Jake than she meant to. Her only option, though, was to fall on the floor.

"You look beautiful," Jake whispered.

"Thanks," Beth said. "You too." She felt too confused to even know what she was saying. To her great relief, the waitress appeared almost immediately. "Hot chocolate, please," Beth said. "With extra whipped cream."

"I'll have the same," Jake said.

Beth felt a sense of satisfaction at the surprise that was so plain on Kimmy and Michelle's faces. Whether it was because of the way Beth was dressed or the way Jake was treating her she wasn't sure. But it made her smile even brighter.

The conversation soon turned to snowboarding. Jake had convinced his mom to get him a new board that morning, and he had gone with Nick and Scott to try it out.

"You should have seen him!" Nick said, pointing to Jake. "He did a 450-degree!"

"Wow, that's fantastic!" Kimmy said, smiling at Jake.

"Yeah," Michelle added. "What is it?"

Beth wanted to laugh at Michelle's ignorance, but she also felt her stomach knot. So Jake had done the 450? She wanted to be happy for him, but she was enough of a competitor to be a little bit worried.

"It's a spin, Michelle," she said. "You spin one and a half times in the air and ski backwards. It's really tough to do." She took a deep breath and said, "That's great, Jake."

Jake looked very proud of himself until Nick added, "Yeah, he looked great until he fell over backwards into a ditch!"

Beth felt a flash of relief that Jake hadn't managed to stay up, but then immediately felt guilty.

"So, Beth," Jake anxiously changed the subject, "are you going to the Winter Carnival Dance?"

"No," she said, "I don't usually go to that kind of thing."

"Beth, you should come," Nick said. "A big group of us usually goes."

Beth looked at Jake, who looked a little annoyed with Nick, but he said, "Yeah, come with our group."

Before Beth could say anything, Kimmy and Michelle hopped into the conversation, talking about the dresses they were going to wear. Beth was relieved to be left out of the conversation for a while.

Later, after devouring burgers and drinking another round of hot chocolate, Beth started to relax a little and enjoy their kidding around. Even Kimmy and Michelle were funny, although it was usually unintentional. Some of the stories and jokes Nick and Scott told were a little "off-color," as Beth's mom would say. Beth laughed because everyone else did. But she was surprisingly relieved when the check came.

She reached for her ticket, but Jake put his hand over hers, stopping her. "My treat," he said, pulling out a twenty-dollar bill. Beth's hand still felt the warmth of Jake's, even when he took it away to hand the money to the waitress.

It was dark when they left the restaurant. Beth looked for Mrs. Bahlman's car. "Where's your mom?" she asked.

"I told her to pick me up in front of your house," he said. "I thought it would be nice to walk from here."

The stars were beautiful, and the night was crisp but not too cold. Beth and Jake walked close to each other, and their arms brushed occasionally. Beth wondered if he would hold her hand and wasn't sure whether she wanted him to or not.

As they turned the corner, Beth heard Kimmy and Michelle's voices drifting down the street.

"Did you see how Jake looked at her tonight?" Kimmy said.

"Don't worry, Kim," Michelle said. "You know he doesn't go for the board-broad types."

Board broad was one of Beth's least favorite terms. It referred to a female who snowboarded. Beth heard their voices grow faint. She felt awkward. Had Jake heard? If he had, he didn't act like it.

"Are you going to the slopes tomorrow?" he asked.

"I don't know. I'll have to check with my dad."

"Maybe I'll see you there," he said.

After that they walked in silence. Beth wished she could figure out whether Jake liked her or not. Was she just fun for him to hang out with? Or was it something more?

At her front door she said good-night. "Thanks for dinner," she said. "I had a really nice time."

"Me too," he said softly. "See you later, Beth Summers."

He squeezed her hand and then quickly walked back to the street where his mother's car had just pulled up. He got in, but the car idled while Beth fumbled for her front door key. She was shaking, and it took twice as long as usual to get the key to turn in the lock. Finally, when she opened the front door, Mrs. Bahlman's car pulled away. *Well*, thought Beth, remembering Jake's hand on hers, *I guess that answers that question.*

CHAPTER:04

Sunday dawned bright and clear. Beth buried her head in her pillow to keep out the sunlight, and wondered if her dad would take them to church that morning. She didn't hear any sounds anywhere else in the house, so she figured they must be staying home. Her dad went through spells when he thought it would be "good" if they all went to church together, but just as often he said he was too tired or busy or stressed, and they stayed home.

Beth was relieved. She'd stayed awake a long time the night before, trying to figure out how she felt about Jake. She was thrilled to know that he really did like her. It felt great that maybe she actually was pretty enough, or cool enough, for a guy like Jake. But did she really like him? She wasn't totally sure.

Plus she felt a little guilty about missing church. She rolled over on her back and stared at the ceiling.

"Good morning, God," she prayed. "I guess we're

not going to church this morning, but I hope it's OK that I still talk to you. Thanks for this beautiful day, and . . . " She paused. Should she talk to God about Jake? Was that way too weird? "And thanks that I had such a nice time with Jake. Please help him to like me and help me to know if I like him. Amen."

Around eleven o'clock, Jake called and asked if Beth could come to the slopes with him that afternoon.

"I'll have to ask my dad," she said, dreading that already.

But when she asked her father, he just grunted and said, "Fine. If you want to be a slacker, hang out with your slacker friends. Just be home in time for dinner. Your mom's got a pot roast in the oven."

Beth couldn't believe it was that easy. After she told Jake and hung up the phone, she dressed in her snow gear and grabbed her new snowboard.

The phone rang. For a moment, Beth was afraid Jake was calling to cancel on her.

"Hello," she said.

"Hey!" Brooke said. "We just finished with our campus fellowship service, and I think Ty and I are going skiing. No training. Just for fun. Wanna come?"

"Actually," Beth said, "I'm getting ready to leave right now." Beth felt weird telling her about going with Jake, but Brooke didn't seem to mind.

"No problem. We'll see you there."

Just then, Jake's mom honked the horn. Beth hurried out the front door, careful not to nick anything with her board. Jake got out and opened the door for her. He'd never done anything like that before. Beth remembered last night and blushed.

"Hey," Jake said smiling.

"Hey," Beth replied, staring at her boots. "Hi, Mrs. Bahlman," she added. "Thanks for picking me up."

"You're welcome, Beth," Jake's mom said.

She later dropped them off in the Devil's Head parking lot. Beth realized that soon she'd be alone with Jake. OK, alone at a packed ski resort. But she felt awkward and didn't say anything at all as they grabbed their gear and headed into the Cliffhaus, the main lodge. Jake was quiet too.

"I had a really nice time last night," he said at last.

"Yeah, me too," she said, glad to have something to say. "Great time." *What an idiot!* she thought. *What am I even saying?*

"You know," Jake said, pointing to the lodge, "it would make so much more sense to have a restaurant inside the Cliffhaus instead of over by the Alley."

"Absolutely," Beth said. "I've always thought so too."

She knew she had never given it a thought in her life until now, but she was too nervous to even think about what she was saying.

Beth looked up toward the chalet-style lodge,

with its black, metal A-frame structure and large windowpanes. The black metal was a stark contrast to the thick, white snow. As they approached the front door, Beth looked over at the slopes to see skiers and snowboarders riding the lifts up. She couldn't wait to get her boots on and head up the mountain.

"I'll meet you out here," Jake said, pointing to the lobby area as they headed for the changing rooms.

"Great," Beth said. "I'll only need a few minutes."

Once inside the locker room, Beth shoved her sweatshirt, shoes, and a pair of sweats inside a locker. Then she looked in the mirror to check her makeup. She hadn't risked putting very much on because she didn't want to make her father mad. But it did help make her look a little older. As she stared at her reflection, she thought that she might be *almost* pretty.

She looked at her body covered in a heavy coat and ski pants. Kimmy and Michelle had both said they hated to ski because the coats made them look so fat. How shallow was that?

As she and Jake rode the ski lift up the hill, she looked out over Devil's Alley. It was considered a difficult run. Once a man had stopped her as she was about to ski down it to make sure she wasn't trying the wrong run. But she had mastered the Alley on skis when she was eleven years old. Back in those days, her dad would ski with her and guide her through the course. But it was also on the Alley where she saw her first snowboard rider. She was hooked from that moment on. She loved the speed and the freedom of not using poles.

Her dad had long since stopped coming to the slopes with her. Suddenly, she felt really sad. She missed those times with her dad. Maybe if she'd never tried snowboarding, things would be different between them.

She shook her head and tried to focus on what was happening right then. *I'm riding on a ski lift alone with the most popular boy in school, who told me I'm pretty. It can't get any better than this!*

At the top of the slope, Beth snapped into her bindings with one click of her heel. Jake had older bindings that he needed to manually strap. Beth reached for her helmet and laughed.

"What?" Jake asked.

"Nothing," she said. "It's just that Kimmy and Michelle said one of the many reasons they would never snowboard is that helmets would mess up their hair."

Jake didn't laugh. "Kimmy and Michelle think it's important to look nice. I guess there's nothing wrong with that."

Great, she thought. *He's mad at me because I made fun of his friends. I've ruined the afternoon.*

With their boards secure and their safety gear on, Beth and Jake dropped into the run. Before long they were at the jumping platform, and Beth shot ahead to successfully complete a 450-degree jump. Jake avoided the jump and moved around so that when Beth touched ground, they could finish the run together.

After a couple of really great runs, Jake said, "Let's go get a burger at the Avalanche Grill."

Beth wasn't hungry, but she didn't want to disagree with him, so they made their way across Cauldron's Cutoff, a novice course, and right onto the side deck of the grill. Snapping off their bindings and pulling locks from their pockets, they used the chains that were welded onto the rack to lock their boards and helmets to the wall outside.

The cozy warmth of the Avalanche was a shock to Beth's glowing cheeks as they came in from the cold. They found a table next to the fireplace and sat down. Jake went back to get in line for food while Beth warmed her hands and laid her gloves out on the raised hearth. By the time he came back with their lunches, Beth was completely defrosted—and starved.

Beth was worried that things would be weird, but soon they were talking as easily as ever. Jake asked her all about Brooke. He wanted to know how Brooke had become such an excellent skier.

"Dad was a great skier," she said, "and everyone thought he'd make the Olympic team. Then he injured his knee and had to drop out of the program. He started Brooke and me on the bunny slope when each of us turned four, and by the time we were seven, we were skiing down the intermediate slopes."

"Wow," Jake said. "It must be great to get that kind of coaching."

"It has its drawbacks," Beth said. "My dad hates the fact that I snowboard. He always wanted me to be a skier like Brooke . . . and like him."

"What about snowboarding part of the time and skiing the other part?" Jake suggested.

"Jake," Beth tried to explain, "I'm not graceful like my sister. She can ski and look so casual and confident—even in tricky spots. I'm a klutz on skis. But when I ride a board, it's faster, a little sloppier, and honestly, if you fall, the judges are more forgiving."

"Maybe he'll come around," Jake said.

Beth sighed. "Not a chance."

"Maybe you should just give up snowboarding," Jake said.

Beth's eyes shot up at him. Was he serious? He caught her glance and grinned.

"Just kidding," he said.

Beth shrugged. But Jake reached for her hand and squeezed it. She couldn't help but wish Michelle and Kimmy would walk in and see her sitting with Jake. Instead, she saw Brooke and her boyfriend Ty walking in. Beth waved, and Brooke and Ty came toward them.

Brooke was stopped by a ten-year-old girl who wanted her autograph. When they finally reached Beth and Jake's table, Beth asked, "What have you two been up to this morning?"

It was a good question. They both looked like they'd fallen in the snow a couple of times, unusual for such expert skiers.

"The Outer Limits was empty," Brooke said, "so Ty wanted to do some runs over there."

"You're kidding," Jake said. "That's the most difficult slope on the mountain. Is it safe?"

"If you're careful," Beth answered.

"You've done the Outer Limits?" Jake asked her, noticeably surprised. "I never even tried the *Alley* until I was with you and Brooke."

"It's such a rush!" Beth added. "You push off the edge, and it takes you straight down the mountain. The jump at the end sends you forty feet in the air."

Beth couldn't figure out the look on Jake's face. He looked impressed, but also—she wasn't really sure what—mad, maybe?

"Brooke," Ty said, "I'm starved. You ready to grab some lunch?"

"You think I could handle it?" Jake asked.

"I don't know," Ty said. "The chili cheeseburgers can be a little intense."

"No," Jake said, "I mean the Outer Limits."

"No offense, dude," Ty answered, "but if you've just been doing the Alley for a week or so, you need to get totally comfortable on that first. The Outer Limits is pretty much a pro course."

Brooke and Ty said good-bye and went to stand in the lunch line.

"Man," Jake said under his breath, "I would *so* love to try it."

Beth paused. Should she really say this? "I'll take you down it sometime soon," she told him.

"Really? Cool!"

They finished their lunch, and Beth grabbed her gloves and goggles from the hearth. As they walked out, they passed a board with notices of skis and snowboards for sale, college students offering ski lessons, free puppies, and cross-country skiing guides. Most of them had been there awhile and looked pretty ragged.

But a large notice posted in the center caught their attention. Winter Carnival was coming up. The poster announced that, for the first time, there would be a Carnival Teen Open for snowboarders ages twelve to eighteen.

"Wow," Beth said. "You think you might go out for it?"

"I'd love to," he said.

"Me too," Beth said.

Jake turned and looked at her for a moment, but didn't say anything. He was still acting strangely. Beth was ready to get back on the slopes where they didn't have as much reason to talk.

"Hey," Beth said, "we've got time for at least three more good runs before your mom picks us up."

"Where do you want to go?" Jake asked.

"Where would *you* like to go?" Beth asked.

"The Outer Limits," he said without hesitation.

Beth wasn't so sure, but she hated to say no.

"You said you'd take me sometime soon," Jake continued. "But if you don't think I'm good enough just because I'm not one of you Summers girls—" Jake sounded angry.

"You have to promise me you'll take it slow the first time and just follow my lead," Beth insisted.

"No problem," Jake said, relaxing a little. "Anything you say."

"Let's go then," Beth said. A little shiver of fear raced down her spine. What if Jake got hurt? But she shook off the feeling. He was a natural.

Jake realized as they left the building that the Outer Limits was on the other side of the mountain.

"How are we going to get there?" Jake asked.

"We'll take the number two lift up and then board down to the Revenge run. Once we're there, we can drop down through the Way Over trail and we're there."

"Sounds good to me," Jake said.

They headed for the lift, just a hundred yards from the Avalanche Grill. After snowboarding down the upper trails, they stood at the edge of the Outer Limits, catching their breath. To less experienced skiers, it looked like a sheer drop down the mountain.

"You sure you're ready for this?" Beth said, regretting that she'd agreed to bring Jake here.

"Watch me!" he said angrily and dropped down the slope.

Beth's stomach was in her throat, afraid of what could happen to him, but she quickly followed his lead. To Jake's credit, he didn't do anything stupid and crisscrossed the slope to slow down his speed.

"You're doing great!" Beth yelled, and Jake grinned. But he had taken his eyes off the snow for a split second and tumbled end over end until he stopped near a tree.

Beth sped over to him on her board. "You OK?"

Jake wiped snow off his goggles and scrambled

back up. "Yeah, no problem. Next time, don't talk to me on the slopes."

His words stung. "Sorry," she said. "Maybe we should finish the run and head over to one of the other trails."

"No way!" Jake said and pushed off down the mountain again.

They spent the next two hours in silence, conquering the Outer Limits. Beth was impressed. Even though Jake was cocky, he really paid attention to her instructions and did well. He fell another couple of times, but he always got back up.

"Do you think any of the other kids going out for the Open have ever done the Outer Limits?" he asked her as they headed back to the lodge.

"Probably not," Beth said. *And who cares?* she thought. *The Open won't come near this part of the mountain.*

When Mrs. Bahlman pulled up at the lodge turnaround, Beth and Jake were both ready to call it a day. The ride home was quiet. Beth wondered what Jake was thinking. He'd acted really strange all day. Sometimes he seemed almost angry at Beth. But on the way home, he actually reached over and held her hand. She felt sort of stupid because she still had her gloves on. But it was kind of nice.

When she got home, she peeled off her ski jacket

and threw herself on the bed. She wondered what she had done to make Jake angry on the slopes. She decided not to worry about it. Maybe he was just nervous and mad at himself for falling. Beth was almost asleep when Brooke opened her bedroom door.

"Hey," Brooke whispered, "can I come in?"

"Sure," Beth said groggily. "What's up?"

"I just wanted to see how your day went."

"Good," Beth said, her smile growing as she thought more about it.

"He's pretty cute," Brooke offered.

"Yeah."

"Talked to Reed lately?" Brooke asked.

"Not much," Beth said groggily.

Brooke's eyebrows pushed together the way they did when something was bothering her. But all she said was, "Well, sleep tight. I'm heading back to school, but I'll see you next weekend." Then she bent down to give her sister a kiss on the forehead.

CHAPTER:05

The next morning, Beth raided Brooke's closet again. Her sister had left most of her nicer clothes at home. Brooke's dorm closet was small, and she mostly wore jeans and sweatshirts on campus anyway. Beth thought that was fine for Brooke, who would look like a model in a flannel nightgown. But Beth had really enjoyed how it felt to be noticed at school.

Looking in the mirror, she carefully applied as much makeup as she thought she could get away with and was pleased with the final result. She left the house feeling confident it was going to be a great week.

As she walked down the main corridor of school, hoping to see Jake, she ran into Reed—literally.

"Whoa!" he said, turning away so his orange juice didn't spill all over her.

"Sorry," she said.

Reed looked at her intensely before asking, "How was your weekend?"

"Fine," she said. She wasn't really in the mood to talk to Reed about Jake. "What about you?"

"Fine," Reed answered. "Missed you at youth group last night."

Suddenly, Beth remembered her promise to call Reed. "Oh, Reed, I'm so sorry. I meant to let you know. Jake called and wanted to go boarding and—"

"Jake," Reed said. "Yeah, I guess I should have known."

"What's that supposed to mean?"

"Look at you," he said. "You've turned into a Kimmy clone. You've been hanging out with them for a week, and you don't even look like yourself anymore."

"Just because I want to wear nice clothes and put on a little lip gloss—"

"A *gallon* of lip gloss," Reed said. "I don't care. But I do care that you're blowing me off to hang out with those clothes hangers."

"Can't I be your friend and their friend too?"

Reed paused. "I'm not sure," he said. Then he turned and walked away.

Hot tears pooled in Beth's eyes, but she didn't cry. She was losing her best friend, and it really hurt. Dragging her feet, she walked to her locker, where Jake waited for her.

Beth forced herself to smile. "So," she said, "I had

a great time on the slopes yesterday. When do you want us to go again?"

"Actually," he said slowly, "I'm not sure."

"Don't you want to practice for the Teen Open?" she asked. She hoped he was serious about planning to compete, but even more she wanted the chance to get ready for it herself.

"Well," Jake said, "I probably should. It's just . . ."

"Just what?" Beth asked, confused.

"You know that Scottie and Michelle are going together, and so are Nick and Kimmy," Jake explained. "Scottie and Nick are practicing for the Open, and the girls want to cheer the guys on."

"That's fine," Beth said, thinking he was worried she wouldn't want to snowboard in front of Kimmy and Michelle. "They can."

"Well," Jake said slowly, "it's just that it would be cool for me to have a girlfriend there cheering me on."

Beth felt a weird confusion creep over her. What did Jake mean?

"Are you saying you want me to be your girl-friend?" Beth asked.

"I'm saying I kind of thought you already were."

"Um . . . OK then," Beth said.

"OK? You're OK with all that?"

Now Beth was more confused. Why didn't he think she'd be OK with being his girlfriend?

"Of course I am," she said. "Why shouldn't I be?"

"It's just that I thought you might want to enter the Open, and . . ."

"Oh," Beth said. Now she understood. Jake wanted a girlfriend like Michelle or Kimmy—one who cheered for him on the sidelines instead of competing against him on the slopes.

"Oh," Beth said again, a knot forming in her stomach. "I don't know, Jake. I'll . . . have to think about it."

"Fine, Beth," he said, but he sounded angry. "If you have to think about whether or not you want to support me, then maybe Kimmy and Michelle were right. Maybe you're not mature enough to be my girlfriend." He turned and walked away.

Beth stood frozen. Is that what they thought? That she was just some little kid?

"Wait, Jake," she said, and he stopped. "Of course I want to cheer for you. It's just . . ." Could she really give up the Open for Jake? She looked at him and thought how cute he was, how great it felt holding his hand, having people look at her and know that she was Jake's girl. But still . . . the Open was huge. "Give me a couple of days to think about it."

Jake didn't smile, but he didn't look so angry. "OK," he said. "I'll be waiting."

That afternoon her dad's car was in the driveway when she got home from school, which never happened unless her dad had a migraine or something. She let herself in quietly and went to the kitchen to grab a snack. Her dad was sitting at the kitchen table, going over information about the Olympics for Brooke.

Beth fixed herself a bowl of cornflakes. "If you're going to train as a serious athlete," her dad said, "that's not the kind of meal you need. But, I forgot. You just want to mess around on your snowboard."

Beth started to argue, but she noticed how pale he looked. She swallowed her anger and said, "You feel OK?"

"Yes," he said. "No. I don't know. Sit down, Beth."

Beth had no idea what was going on, but she immediately obeyed.

After a moment he said, "I got laid off today."

"What?" she asked in shock. "But you've been working so hard lately!"

"The agency had a huge account that was threatening to walk away. My department put in tons of extra hours to keep the client happy. But instead, some big Chicago agency took it from us. My whole department has been laid off."

Beth felt sick. As much as her dad's criticism could hurt her, she hated to see him like this. But she didn't know what to do or say.

"I'm sorry, Daddy," she said. "Is there anything I can do?"

"Just leave me alone right now, Beth," he said. "I just really want to be alone."

Beth did what he asked and went to her room. She felt helpless and a little scared. What would they do if her dad couldn't find a job?

She lay on her bed and stared at the ceiling, thinking about Jake, her dad, and the Open. *What should I do, Lord?* she prayed silently. She thought about how happy it would make Jake if she stood on the sidelines to cheer for him. *Please help me make a wise choice.* By the time she started her homework, she had made a decision.

Beth walked down the hall, trying hard not to fall on her face in the heels she'd borrowed from Brooke. It was hard to balance.

"Hey," Reed said, snapping Beth out of her trance.

"Hey," she said, wondering whether he was still mad at her.

"What's with the schoolgirl look, Britney?" he said.

Beth looked down at the short plaid skirt and fitted blouse she was wearing. Maybe it was a little bit too much. But she didn't want to admit that to Reed.

"I just wanted to try something new," she said.

"You wanted it, or Jake did?" Reed asked.

"What's that supposed to mean?" Beth snapped defensively.

"That I've lost my best friend to a guy who's known for using people," Reed said. "He did it to me the day we ran into you and Brooke on the hill. Ian told me he only invited me so he could use my new deck."

"So you think no guy in his right mind could possibly like me for myself?" Beth asked. "What would he be using me for?"

"Hmm . . . let me think," Reed said sarcastically.

Beth tensed, but chose to ignore the comment and walked away without a word. Reed hated Jake and couldn't believe that Jake could actually like her for who she was. All Reed wanted to do was play video games and read comic books. He just wasn't as mature as she was.

Her social studies presentation with Kimmy and Michelle was scheduled for that Friday. When they broke into groups to discuss their presentations, Kimmy and Michelle both stared blankly at Beth. Then Beth had a stroke of brilliance.

"Why don't we dress up?" she asked. She thought if she could get those girls to do anything well, that would be it.

"As what?" Kimmy asked.

Beth thought for a moment. "You two could be princesses," Beth said.

"Oooh," said Michelle. "I have the perfect outfit. I'll look just like the girl from *The Princess Diaries*."

"Michelle," Beth said, "you'll need to dress up like a *medieval* princess."

"Oh yeah," said Kimmy, "like with the pointy hats and stuff?"

"Exactly," Beth said.

"What about you, Beth?" Michelle asked. "What will you wear?"

Beth hadn't thought that far yet. "I think I'll just be the narrator," she said.

At lunch, she didn't even bother to look for where Reed was sitting. She went straight to Jake's table.

"There you are!" he said as she sat down. "You look great today."

"Thanks," she said. But the compliment didn't feel as good as it should have. Reed's words had spoiled it. *Fine*, she thought. *I'll just stop paying attention to anything Reed says.*

"So, Beth," Kimmy said, "are you coming on Sunday to cheer the guys at the slopes?"

"Yeah," Michelle said, "we're all going to dress alike and be a cheerleading squad for the guys."

Beth was about to answer, when everything at the

table got very quiet. Jake stared at her intensely. Now was the moment to let him know her decision.

"Do you have an extra outfit for me?" Beth asked. "I'd love to come and cheer the guys on."

Even as she said it, she wondered whether she was telling the complete truth. Would she really love to? No. What she'd love to do was be out on the slopes preparing for the Open. But she'd made up her mind. She looked over at a grinning Jake.

"Guys," he said to Nick and Scottie, "you don't have a chance. With Beth cheering for me, I can't lose."

"She'd be more help if she were *coaching* you," Scottie said.

Beth was surprised. She hadn't thought of it that way. Then, at least, she could still be on the slopes. "Would you like me to?"

"Well, now that I've conquered the Outer Limits," Jake said, "I don't know what else I need to learn. But I guess it couldn't hurt. Sure, why not?"

Beth was a little annoyed that he didn't tell anyone that *she* was the one who showed him how to board the Outer Limits. But she didn't have a chance to say anything, because Scottie and Nick were full of questions about Jake's new accomplishment. They made plans to hit the slopes that afternoon.

When Beth heard Mrs. Bahlman's horn honk in

her driveway that afternoon, she grabbed her boots and her board, her helmet and gloves.

"Hey, Mrs. Bahlman," Beth said, climbing in.

"Hi, Beth," Jake's mother said. "Ready to help my son for the Open?"

"You bet," Beth said, feeling a little sick inside.

Jake smiled at Beth, and his smile made her hands shake a little.

"Hey, snow bunny," Jake said and squeezed her hand.

Nick, Kimmy, Michelle, and Scottie were in the back already. Beth noticed that Ian wasn't with them.

"No Ian?" Beth asked.

"Nah, he's been hanging around with your geeky friend instead," Jake said. "But we got all of our video shoots done with him, so we don't need him anymore."

Geeky friend? thought Beth. *He must mean Reed!* For a minute she thought about rushing to Reed's defense. Reed wasn't a geek. He just didn't feel like he had to like the same things as everyone else to be cool.

But then Beth remembered how Reed had treated her. Maybe it *was* kind of geeky to spend your afternoons at Atomic Comics. So she kept her mouth shut and rode in silence to the slopes.

Kimmy and Michelle stayed in the lodge drinking

hot chocolate while Beth and the guys hit the slopes. She was surprised by how much she enjoyed teaching them. They were all pretty decent boarders, especially for just getting into it this winter. But she knew some of the really hard competitive techniques they'd never heard of.

Scottie said it was cool when Beth did her "verts," shooting up the half-pipes just like he did at the skate park in the summer. Nick asked her to show him how to do a Superman forward flip, but she told him she was afraid to even try a simple back flip off the ramps.

"Trust me, guys, it's all about the grabs," Beth explained with authority. "When you jump, you have to tuck in and grab board."

It got dark quickly, so they headed back to the lodge to get Kimmy and Michelle.

"That was great," Jake said. "We can practice every day after school this week, and all day Saturday and Sunday."

Kimmy pointed to a sign above the entryway. "You won't be practicing this Sunday," she said.

"Why not?" Jake said.

"There's some women's downhill snowboard competition here," she replied.

"Oh, that's right," Beth said. "Natty LeBatt is competing."

"Who's that?" Kimmy asked.

"She's the Canadian women's Olympic snowboard champion," Beth said, bugged that none of them even knew the name of one of her idols.

"Oh, so a board broad?" Michelle said.

"Yeah, I guess, if you want to put it that way," Beth answered.

"You used to look like a board broad," Michelle said, "but you way don't anymore. You look almost pretty now."

Beth seethed inside. Even Jake looked at Michelle as if she'd gone too far.

"Beth's a great boarder and one of the prettiest girls I know," he said.

Beth's stomach did a flip. A good boarder *and* pretty? She and Jake smiled at one another, while Michelle just looked confused.

CHAPTER:06

Since Brooke had an appointment with her physical therapist that afternoon, she stayed in town to spend the evening with Beth.

"What's wrong?" Brooke asked as they sat on the couch together. "You're really quiet tonight."

Beth was thinking about so many things that she didn't know where to start.

"It's Dad," she said, choosing the most obvious. "I'm just really worried about him. What if he can't find another job?"

"I know," Brooke said. "I've been thinking a lot about him too. We just have to trust that God has a plan in all of this. The people in my Bible study group are praying for him."

"Do you really think that, Brooke?" Beth asked. "That God has a plan for everything? Because if he does, I think some of his plans are pretty lousy."

Beth was afraid Brooke would be mad that she

said something mean about God, but Brooke just laughed.

"I've felt that way sometimes too," she said. "But the Bible says that all things work together for good for people who love and follow God."

"Then why do so many bad things happen?" Beth asked.

"God doesn't promise that everything will always *be* good," Brooke said. "Just that he will use it *for* our good."

"What's so good about dad losing his job?" Beth asked.

"I don't know yet," Brooke answered. "But I believe that God will bring something good out of it."

It was still a little strange to Beth that Brooke had such a strong faith. She didn't talk about God much before she went to college, but since she'd gotten involved in her campus fellowship, God seemed really important to her.

"Stop," Beth said as Brooke flipped through all the channels again. The Extreme Channel was showing a replay of a men's snowboarding championship. Natty LeBatt, Beth's hero, was one of the commentators.

Rich Gordon, whom his fans called Flash, was leading in a race of four snowboarders, up and over slopes and into trenches. As Gordon crossed the finish line a good ten yards ahead of the second-place boarder, the cameras focused in on a pretty blonde girl on the sidelines, who was jumping up and down and screaming. Within moments, Natty LeBatt was standing in front of Gordon and telling the viewers she was about to interview the champion. As he pulled off his helmet, that same blonde woman from the sidelines came running over and hugged him. He turned and kissed her.

"Who is this, Rich?" Natty asked.

"This is my fiancé Lisa," Rich said with pride. "She's been cheering me on since we were in high school."

"Well, Lisa," Natty said, "you must be really proud of Rich."

"Absolutely, Natty," Lisa said with confidence. "Rich is a great rider, and he has a knack for navigating terrain even on the first time through a course. He's been that way since we were in school and raced each other."

"You're a boarder, then?" Natty asked.

"She taught me everything I know," Rich admitted.

"There you have it, folks," Natty interjected as she turned to face the cameras. "Rich and Lisa, you two make a great team."

Brooke turned off the television. "I'd rather be boarding than standing on the sidelines cheering for some guy."

Beth thought it was kind of nice. Maybe someday Jake would say the same thing about her.

"You're awfully quiet," Brooke said a few moments later. "Are you dreaming about winning the Teen Open?"

Beth still hadn't told Brooke about her decision not to enter. "Um, no," Beth said. "I was just thinking about how nice it would be to cheer for someone like that."

"It would be even better to have someone cheer for *you*," Brooke said. "You have so much potential. You're an awesome boarder, Beth. Don't let any guy take that away from you."

"What about Dad?" Beth asked.

"I love Daddy very much, and I'm learning more and more about how important it is to respect him," Brooke said. "But I believe if God gave you the talent you have, then he's great enough to show Dad how much this means to you. Just trust him to work it out."

Beth was glad that Brooke thought she was so talented, but she didn't really want to talk about it anymore. Brooke would flip out when she found Beth wasn't competing in the Open. So Beth decided to put off that moment as long as possible.

Beth continued to train Jake every day after school. She had planned to work with him on each of the runs so that he could get used to every possible obstacle that might come his way the day of the competition. They covered Devil's Alley, the Cyclops, the Serpent's Mogul, and the Lower Serpent run that included a one-hundred-foot pipe formed out of compacted snow on a wood and metal form. Beth was almost positive the competition would take place on that course.

"Tomorrow," Beth said on Friday, "we need to work on your pipe moves."

The big World Civ presentation on Friday went as well as Beth could expect. Kimmy kept calling Michelle "Your Finest" instead of Your Highness, and Michelle almost poked Beth's eye out with the top of her pointy hat, but Beth was pretty sure they got a decent grade. She was just glad to be done with it.

Jake and Beth couldn't practice on Sunday afternoon because of the competition, but Beth didn't mind. Actually, she was relieved to get a break from Jake. He was a good student when the two of them were alone on the slopes, but if Scott or Nick tagged along, all he did was show off. Jake never gave her credit for teaching him everything he knew.

Besides, Brooke had press-box passes for the competition, and she was taking Beth. Beth would get a perfect view of Natty's runs. She was thrilled!

The camera was rolling when the announcer, snowboarding legend Rick Griffith, came up to Brooke. Ty and Beth were standing with her, so Beth couldn't get out of the camera's view without looking goofy.

"Folks," Rick said, "we have a special guest in the booth this afternoon. It's Devil's Head's own Brooke Summers, a college freshman and Olympic hopeful, who has consistently broken records in women's downhill skiing this season. How are you, Brooke?"

If Brooke was nervous, she didn't show it. If anything, Beth thought, she looked calmer and more beautiful than ever. Dad would be proud.

"Hi, Rick. I'm doing great," Brooke responded. "I'm really excited to be here today for the Chalet Women's Invitational. I love to watch these athletes. They have the grace of skaters, the agility of gymnasts, and the maneuverability of skiers."

"Is there anyone in particular you're going to be watching today?" the announcer asked.

"Absolutely, Rick," Brooke replied. "Natalie LeBatt has consistently blown us away with her speed and control. My little sister Beth here has posters of Natty all over her walls."

"Beth," Rick said as he turned his attention to Brooke's younger sister, "are you a boarder too, or do you follow in your sister's ski tracks?"

Beth looked at the announcer and then to her sister. Brooke nodded her head.

"Natty's the best. I board, and I hope to compete against her someday." Beth's voice sounded strange—like it wasn't really even coming out of her mouth. Was she really talking on TV?

"You heard it from the mouths of babes, folks," the announcer said, addressing the camera. "LeBatt is the favorite today. Thanks to Brooke Summers and her sister for coming out today. Brooke, we look forward to seeing you at the next Winter Olympics."

"If I make it there," Brooke said, "I'll be thankful."

"And we'll keep an eye on you, Beth," he said. "This is Rick Griffith for the Extreme Channel. Over to you, Al, at the starting line."

As Beth, Brooke, and Ty walked away from the announcer's booth, Brooke looked at her sister and patted her on the back.

"You did great."

"Thanks," Beth replied.

When they took their heated seats in the enclosed VIP grandstand, a man in a coat carrying a tray of coffee, tea, and hot chocolate made his way to the sisters. Beth was impressed.

"I want to be a VIP more often," she whispered to Ty as Brooke got them some sandwiches.

With a gunshot, the race was on. Natty LeBatt had forced her way to the front of the group of four, squatting forward as she soared down the slight hill. As she came to a mound, she flexed her knees and took it without her board even leaving the ground. Just over that mound was a steep drop that led to a jump. LeBatt leaned into the fall and gained even more speed. As she approached the bottom of the slope, she took her board into the jump, sailing outward. Beth watched in amazement as Natty huddled down and held onto her board for less wind resistance.

As Natty touched down, she was already looking into the course to see what was coming. It was a hairpin turn into a pipe. Beth knew that Natty was also an awesome surfer, so the pipe would be interesting to watch. Natty entered the pipe from above, shot down one side, and rode her board straight through to the other side where a ramp had been set up to allow the snowboards to exit the pipe.

The second boarder was a good five yards back. Natty exited the pipe with a jump that took her sailing into the final course, an open area cordoned off with cones, flags, and ropes.

Natty seemed to control her board with wavy hip movements. As she came into the final stretch of downhill run, she again squatted down and zoomed through the finish line. The other competitors came in within five seconds of each other and congratulated Natty with pats on her helmet.

Beth, Brooke, and Ty jumped out of their seats, clapping and cheering. Everyone in the VIP box was cheering as LeBatt came in to talk to the reporters. Beth watched from a distance as Rick Griffith interviewed her.

"What did you think, Beth?" Ty leaned around his girlfriend to ask. "Pretty cool?"

"Totally cool," Beth said with a smile, wishing that Natty would come over and introduce herself.

"She's so good," Brooke commented. "Don't you want to keep working so you can be where she is someday?"

"Yeah, sure, I guess," Beth said. Watching Natty race made Beth think she'd been stupid. Maybe she never should have told Jake she wouldn't race against him.

"You'll have your chance at the Teen Open," Brooke said.

Ty looked surprised. "I didn't think you were competing this year, Beth," he said.

"What are you talking about?" Brooke asked.

"One of my jobs is to organize the registrations," Ty said. "Beth's name isn't anywhere on the list. The only kid from her school is that guy Jake."

Brooke turned and stared at Beth. "Why didn't you register for the Open?"

It was the moment Beth had been dreading. How could she explain all this to Brooke?

"I just thought—" she started.

"Don't *tell* me you let Jake convince you not to race against him," she said.

"Well, actually—" Beth began, but Brooke cut her off again.

"I knew something strange was going on. Beth, how could you?"

"I could and I did, and it's too late to do anything about it now anyway," Beth said. "I was sick of Kimmy and Michelle's snide comments. I wanted to show Jake how important he is to me by cheering for him. And I hated to ask Dad for the registration money after he lost his job."

Brooke shook her head. "I thought you were smarter than this, Beth," she said. "If Jake cared about you, he'd be excited to see you do something well. He wouldn't see it as a threat. Whoever Kimmy and Michelle are, what they think can't be important enough to influence your decision. And as for the money, you know I would have given it to you. You could pay me back after saving up your allowance!"

Beth realized how foolish all her decisions had been. She actually let Kimmy and Michelle decide what was best for her? They couldn't even name the capital of Wisconsin!

Brooke continued, "Beth, you have a gift. God has given you the ability to be a fantastic snowboarder. You should be more concerned about pleasing him than pleasing some girls from your school."

"You're right, Brooke," she said at last, "but it doesn't matter. The registration deadline has passed."

Both Beth and Brooke dropped their heads. But Ty said, "You both seem to be forgetting something. It *might* be that you know someone who could make an exception for a late registration."

"Who?" Beth asked, feeling hopeful again.

"Me, of course!" Ty said.

"Could you?" Beth asked, jumping up.

"No problem at all, Miss Summers," he said.

Beth was thrilled. She realized that this was what she'd wanted all the time. She'd been stupid. And Jake would understand. He really did like her, and if she just explained it to him, everything would be OK.

"There's *one* problem though," Beth said. "I've been training Jake for the last week. I haven't boarded any of the runs myself. I don't know if I can be ready for the Open by next weekend."

"Once again," Ty said, "it's my pleasure to come to your aid. I'll train you myself!"

"Wow," Beth said. "Thanks!" She started to hug Ty, but a beaming Brooke beat her to it.

"We just need a plan," Ty said. And they set to work.

By Monday morning, though, Beth wasn't feeling so confident. What would Jake say when she told him? Did she really want to compete in the Open more than she wanted Jake to like her? When she walked up to her locker, Jake was waiting for her. He handed her a small, gift-wrapped package.

"What's this?" Beth said with an uneasy smile.

"Open it," Jake said.

Beth opened the small box and stared at a beautiful little gold locket shaped like a heart. In it was a small picture of Jake and Beth that Ian must have taken one day at the slopes. Beth looked up at Jake and forced a smile. Would he still want her to have this when he learned she was going to compete in the Open?

"Thanks," Beth said. "It's so pretty. Would you help me put it on?"

After fumbling a little, Jake snapped the necklace into place, and Beth adjusted it. It felt so strange around her neck. But it was reassuring. If Jake could give her a gift like this, surely he cared enough for her to be glad she was going to compete.

She knew she should go ahead and tell him she'd entered the Open. But the bell for first period rang, and he walked away. Beth barely heard a word any of her teachers said that morning. If she wasn't thinking about how she was going to tell Jake about the Open, she was touching her fingers to the necklace. Jewelry, Kimmy and Michelle had said, was serious. What did that mean?

When Beth found herself alone with Jake at the beginning of lunch while the rest of Jake's friends waited for the baked potato bar, she knew it was the time to tell him.

"I'm really excited about the Open," Jake said. "I think I've got a real shot at winning. And it's going to be so terrific having you there to cheer me on. Your smile will be the reason I win."

My coaching will be the reason you win, she thought. *If you win.* Had he always been so cocky? Was she just now noticing it?

"About that," Beth said, taking a deep breath. "There's something I need to tell you."

"Yeah, I know," Jake said. "Those purple hoodies Michelle picked out are pretty hideous—"

"It's not about the hoodies, Jake," Beth said. He was really starting to make her nervous.

"Is it the pom-poms? Don't worry. Those were Kimmy's idea. But I know that's not your style."

"It's not the pom-poms," Beth said. "Please, just let me explain. I've been doing a lot of thinking. I went to see Natty LeBatt board on Sunday. Then I talked to Brooke's boyfriend Ty—"

"What does that have to do with the Open?" Jake asked.

"I'm getting to that," Beth said. "I just realized, watching Natty, how much I love to snowboard."

"Yeah, and you're great at it," Jake said.

"Thanks," Beth continued. "I'm glad you feel that way, because I've decided to compete in the Open."

Jake choked on his chocolate milk. "You're what?" he said, coughing. "But you promised! You told me you'd be there cheering me on!"

"I know, Jake. And I'll still be cheering for you— just from the top of the run instead of the bottom."

Jake looked confused and then relieved. "But wait a second. You can't. You already missed the registration deadline!" Beth noticed that he was smiling.

"I know. I thought of that too. But Ty is in charge of registrations, and he asked the officials to make an exception for me."

"But what about your dad? Isn't he going to freak out?" Jake demanded. "I thought you wanted to make him happy."

Beth was starting to wonder whose side Jake was on. "Of course I want my dad to be happy. I want you to be happy too." She thought about Brooke's words and added, "But I also want to use the gift God has given me."

"Do you think God wants you to break your

promise to me?" Jake asked. "All I wanted was one person—*you*—on my side. You said you'd do it. And now you're backing out."

This was going all wrong. Why was he so upset? And was she really breaking a promise to him? She hadn't thought about it that way.

"I'm sorry, Jake," she said. "This is really important to me."

"It's really important to me too," he said. He was quiet for a minute. Then he seemed to relax. "Hey, Beth, forget about it. Do what you want. By the way, are we all still on for the Winter Carnival Dance?"

Jake had mentioned the dance only once before, and he hadn't even asked her to it then. She was pretty sure she'd remember if he had. Usually, if she went at all, she just hung around with Reed and his friends, making fun of all the other kids. Wistfully, she realized that she hadn't laughed nearly as much with Jake as she ever did with Reed.

"So, what about it, Beth?" he said. "Are you going with us?"

"Sure," she said.

Jake changed gears too quickly for her to keep up. For a minute she had been afraid he would break off their friendship. But, evidently, they had just survived their first fight. Beth breathed a sigh of relief.

CHAPTER:07

That afternoon, Ty had to teach a private lesson, and Beth didn't exactly want to ask Jake and his mother for a ride to the slopes. So she decided to take the day off from training and told her mother she was going for a walk.

She paused in front of Reed's house. She hadn't meant to walk that way. Her feet had taken her there automatically. How many afternoons had they spent together, playing video games, building snow forts, studying for tests? And now she had to walk by without even going in. She hadn't spoken to Reed in almost a week. She really missed him. No one else knew her as well as he did.

Hurriedly, Beth walked away. She didn't want the Nagles to see her lurking in the driveway. She had been walking without much purpose, but now her steps grew quicker. She knew what she needed to do.

She stopped two blocks later in front of Atomic Comics, one of Reed's favorite stores. Walking inside, Beth waved to Larry, the shop's owner, who was sitting behind the counter, before heading to the anime section.

"I haven't seen you in a while, Beth," Larry said.

"You know me and winter," Beth said. "It's tough to get some time off the slopes."

"Is your dad coaching you and Brooke?" Larry asked.

"Nope," Beth said with a shrug. "Just Brooke. Although since she's been away at school, not even as much of that."

"So, what can I help you with today?"

"Well," Beth said with some hesitation, "I wanted to get a little something for Reed."

"Can you spend seven bucks?" Larry asked.

"I guess," Beth said. "Why?"

"He didn't have enough to buy all of his Gashopan figures last Friday, and asked me to put one aside for him."

"Sure," Beth said. "Sounds great."

Beth picked up the action figure for Reed, knowing it would be a great peace offering. As she walked out, she almost laughed out loud when she thought of Kimmy and Michelle shopping for comic books. No, they would never be those kinds of friends. So why had she let them have such a big influence on her?

She quickly walked back toward Reed's house, knowing she didn't have much time before her mother would expect her home. Her hands trembled as she rang the doorbell. Mrs. Nagle answered the door and told her Reed was down in the basement.

"Thanks," Beth said as she entered the house and automatically took her shoes off on the rug next to the door. She turned down the hall and opened the door to the basement.

Then she did something that surprised herself. She prayed silently. *Dear God, I really want to still be friends with Reed. Help him to forgive me for being such a jerk. Thanks and amen.*

Reed didn't notice her walk in. He was engrossed in *Donkey Kong*, his favorite game.

"Gotten to level four yet?" she asked.

"Oh," he said coldly, "it's you."

Beth knew she deserved that. She'd treated him badly, but that didn't make her feel any better.

"Yeah, it's me. Can I come in?"

"Looks like you're already in," he said. "How've you been?"

"OK, I guess," she said. "I've been busy training with Ty for the Open."

Beth wasn't sure, but she thought she saw a smile lurking in the corners of Reed's mouth.

"Don't you mean you've been busy training Jake?"

"Yeah," she said, "that too. But I think my days as Jake's coach are over."

"And your days as his girlfriend?" Reed asked.

"Still going," she said. "Although he's not real thrilled with the fact that I'm competing against him at the Open." Unconsciously, she touched the heart pendant.

"Nice necklace," Reed said. "Is it new?"

"Jake gave it to me," she said softly.

Reed looked like he was trying to make up his mind about something. Then he said, "I don't really want to talk about Jake. It never leads us anywhere good. But I just want to say that if I had a girl who could snowboard as well as you, I'd be angry if she *didn't* compete."

"Thanks," Beth said, feeling strangely encouraged. "Hey, I almost forgot. I brought you something." She handed him the bag.

Reed pulled the action figure from the bag. "How did you know?"

"Larry told me," she said.

"You didn't have to get me anything."

"Yes, I did," Beth said. "I needed an excuse to ring your doorbell."

Reed laughed, and they sat down next to each other on the couch. It was great to be with him again. Life just wasn't right without Reed around. They talked about anime night, which was going well. Then Reed told her that a couple of eighth-grade girls— Gina and Jackie—had started coming too. Beth felt a little jealous.

"So you won't be the only female present anymore," Reed said. "That is, if you decide to come back."

"I'll be here Friday," she promised.

"That's fine, but you won't find anyone else here," Reed says. "We're all going together to the dance at school. It may not be as cool as anime night, but we don't want to be snobs."

Beth smiled. "The dance had slipped my mind."

Reed added, "You're welcome to join us, unless . . ."

"Thanks, but yeah, I'm going with Jake's group," Beth said.

"Sure," Reed said. "Of course." He looked a little disappointed, but he went on. "Next Friday then. We'll be watching *Kaiju Big Battel*."

"I wouldn't miss it."

Since it was now dark outside and the temperature had dropped, Mrs. Nagle offered to give Beth a ride home.

"It's great seeing you again, Beth," Mrs. Nagle said as they got in the car. "You haven't been around much lately."

"Mrs. Nagle," Beth said, "may I ask you a question?"

"Of course, Beth. Anything you want."

Beth swallowed. She wasn't used to talking to anyone about this sort of thing. But she thought Mrs. Nagle was the one to ask. "When you pray, how do you know God is listening?"

"Oh," Mrs. Nagle replied. She seemed a little surprised, but quickly recovered. "That's hard to say. I suppose I don't always *feel* like he's listening. I just trust that he is, because that's what he promised to do."

"I guess what I mean is, how do you know when God is speaking to you? When you pray for something and you think you have an answer, how do you know that answer is from God?" Beth was speaking so quickly that she ran out of breath.

"Hmm. The way God talks to us is personal, and a little hard to explain. But if I'm not sure what I'm thinking is coming from God, I check other places I know I can trust. Kind of like getting confirmation."

"Like what?" Beth asked.

"Like the Bible, first of all. If what I'm thinking or doing is out of line with what the Bible says, then I know I'm wrong, because God never contradicts himself."

Beth had no idea where to find in the Bible whether she should compete in the Open or cheer for Jake on the sidelines.

"What if what you're asking God about isn't dealt with, specifically, in the Bible?" Beth asked.

Beth had prayed before deciding not to compete in the Open, and she thought she was making the right decision. But now she had decided that she *would* compete. Which was right? And by changing her mind, was she lying to Jake?

"It's hard without knowing the specifics," Mrs. Nagle began, "but when you're confused, a good place to start is by asking people who have been Christians awhile and who are living wise, godly lives. They won't always know the right answers, but sometimes they can give you a different perspective."

Did that mean she should listen to Brooke instead of Jake?

"Thanks, Mrs. Nagle," Beth said.

Beth must have still looked concerned, because Mrs. Nagle added, "Remember that the Bible tells us that all things work together for good for people who are striving to love and follow God. So even if you make a bad decision, God can teach you a lesson through it."

"Yeah," Beth said "my sister said kind of the same thing."

"Then you're blessed to have a sister like that," Mrs. Nagle said as she pulled into Beth's driveway. "Here you are."

"Thanks," Beth said, getting out of the car. "You really helped a lot."

Fortunately, Beth didn't have much homework that night. She decided to check her e-mail. Brooke was online and sent Beth an instant message, asking how things went with Jake.

"Fine," Beth wrote. "He was kind of upset at first, but then he seemed to be OK."

"You guys still friends?" Brooke wrote.

"Yeah," Beth replied. "He gave me a really pretty necklace."

"Was that before or after you told him?"

"Before," Beth answered.

For a few moments, there was no reply. Then Brooke wrote, "So, have you talked to Reed much lately?"

"Yep. Saw him tonight."

"What does he think about Jake?" Brooke asked.

"Not much," Beth wrote. "He thinks Jake should be glad that I'm competing."

"I always liked that kid," Brooke replied. "Why didn't you two ever . . . you know, become a thing?"

"Are you crazy? I've known him since kindergarten. I think all that time in the cold has frozen your brain."

"Maybe so," Brooke answered.

Then Beth's sister wrote that she had a test in

world literature she needed to be studying for, and that reminded Beth she had a little homework too, so they signed off.

That night, as she snuggled under her warm down comforter, Beth silently prayed, *God, I'm sorry if I made a bad decision before. I felt like I was doing the right thing to give up the Open—that it was a way to show Jake and Daddy how much I cared about them. Then Brooke and Ty got me so excited about competing that I said yes without thinking about the fact that I was going back on what I told Jake.*

So, maybe I was wrong at first, and then wrong again. Now I don't know what to do! I don't know enough about the Bible to know where to look or what to read. But I think I'd like to get to know you better, and I'd really like your help knowing how to handle the mess I've made of things. Thanks. Amen.

The next day at lunch Beth didn't even see Jake in the cafeteria. That was OK. She wanted to sit with Reed anyway and make sure they were OK.

Beth had sat with Reed almost every day for lunch for their entire school careers. But today, as she walked across the cafeteria to his table, for some reason it drew stares.

"Why is everyone looking at me?" she whispered to Reed as she slid onto the bench beside him.

"Because Jake Bahlman's girl does not usually sit

with Reed Nagle, president of the Anime Club," he said.

"I guess there's a first time for everything," she replied.

She noticed some new faces among the usual crowd Reed hung out with—the two new girl members in the Anime Club. An Asian girl named Gina with a stripe of blue hair in each of her pigtails sat across from Reed. Beth looked at her closely. She was wearing a Natty LeBatt T-shirt.

"Do you board?" Beth asked.

"I'm learning," Gina said.

"We should go to the slopes together sometime," Beth said.

The other girl's name was Jackie. She was wearing a Mighty Atom T-shirt and had a cool denim jacket on over it. Suddenly, Beth felt overdressed and ridiculous in her makeup and jewelry. She'd be much more comfortable dressed like Jackie or Gina.

Beth realized she was staring at Jackie, so she said, "Nice jacket."

"Thanks," Jackie said. "I love your heart necklace. Did your parents give it to you?"

Reed snorted, and Beth just said, "No." Thankfully, Jackie didn't pursue it.

Beth had forgotten how much she could laugh when she was around Reed. Jackie and Gina were funny too, and Ian held his own, but Reed made her laugh so hard she couldn't finish her lunch. The other girls kept saying what a great guy Reed was, and it made Beth a little uncomfortable. She wasn't used to sharing Reed with other girls. But she felt stupid for even thinking that. After all, she had no claims on him.

CHAPTER:08

In the middle of the week, Beth arranged to meet Ty at the slopes for more practice. Brooke came home so she could drive Beth. They pulled in to the hotel parking lot on the far side of the resort. Ty was waiting for them when they got there.

Beth was confused as to why they were meeting Ty over on this side of the resort, but the answer was soon revealed.

"You've skied or boarded every run at Devil's Head, but you've never attempted the Forbidden Zone," Ty said mysteriously.

"I've never even heard of it," Beth said.

Following Ty, they crossed the parking lot and headed into the snow. Ty pulled out a two-way radio and called for a pickup. In a little less than a minute, the ski patrol pulled up with their snowmobiles, ready to take the sisters and Ty to the area near a closed gate marked "Future Run Site."

As the snowmobiles came to a stop, Beth got off and looked around. "Has anyone other than employees ever skied or boarded down this run?" Beth asked.

"Just one," Ty said, pointing to Brooke, who waved at her sister.

"This is awesome. It'll let me get a feel for an uncharted course, right?"

"Exactly," Ty said. "But we're not going to waste time. We can get three good runs in today if we stay focused."

Beth and Ty got their boards lined up at the edge of the hill and fastened their helmets in place. Brooke stepped into her ski bindings and prepared to follow them.

"Follow me, Beth," Ty instructed. "We'll take a medium pace the first run down. Next time, you can lead. Third time, if we've got enough light, we'll race. Brooke can fall behind to make sure you're OK. Ready?"

Beth nodded. Ty lowered his visor and dropped onto the intermediate twenty-foot slope. Beth waited five seconds and then followed. Because of his heavier weight, Ty built more speed than Beth and sped ahead.

Soon they came to a fork. Ty pointed Beth toward the right as he steered himself in that direction. The next hundred feet was filled with small mounds in the snow, called moguls, making for a bumpy ride. Then when the two paths again intersected, the snow-covered ground surrounded by trees opened up to reveal a series of orange cones. Ty navigated around each cone and shot out just before another fork.

This time, Ty pointed to the left. Beth followed Ty into the narrow trail, only to discover that not fifty feet into it, there was a natural cliff jump. Ty shot out over the snow-covered hill and held his board as he sailed across the late afternoon sky. Beth was next, and she took the jump like a pro, sailing up and out.

"Woohoo!" she shouted as she flew through the air. Beth hit ground on another slope that appeared to level out just before . . . a drop!

Beth gasped. She watched Ty boarding down what had to be a 70-degree incline. But since she had already dropped in as well, she would have to deal with it. She thought of her helmet with gratitude. It would keep her out of the hospital if she slammed into something.

At the bottom of the course was one last series of small moguls with cones set up to form a path. Ty whipped in and out effortlessly. Beth made it through, but at the expense of several cones. She stopped just a few yards away from the ski patrol snowmobiles that were waiting to take them back up the slope. Brooke skied gracefully downhill and turned to stop herself, causing a spray of snow to hit Ty and his ski patrol buddies.

"That was awesome!" Beth yelled out. "I'm serious. That was incredible."

"You did really well, squirt," Ty said. "Brock and Blake will be impressed."

The twin terrors. But Ty adored them. "Yeah. Tell them hi."

"They'd love to see you," Ty said. "Maybe you can come over for pizza sometime."

That evening, on the drive home, Brooke stopped at the local video rental store and took Beth inside.

"We need *Dance Dance Revolution* for GameBox. Do you guys have it?" Brooke asked.

"Yep," the man said, "we have it. Do you need dance pads?"

"Yes, we do! Thanks," Brooke said.

"What do we need that for?" Beth asked.

"You'll see," Brooke said.

The next stop was the big toy store in town for a hula hoop. Brooke remained mysterious about their purchases.

When they arrived home, Ty had called and left a message for Beth to dance on the *DDR* for an hour that night. He also wanted her to do the hula hoop for a half hour.

"We only have tomorrow, Friday afternoon, and

part of Saturday to get ready," Ty's message said.

"That's OK," Beth said to her sister after the message had played. "I need to practice for the Winter Carnival Dance anyway."

On Friday night, the school gym was decorated in silver and white. The Winter Carnival Dance was the social event of the year at Merrimac Middle School. From the outside, Beth peered into the dark gymnasium to see blue spotlights shining on metallic silver streamers that glistened like icicles as they moved.

The gym was already crowded, but mostly with sixth graders, who didn't know that no one really showed up for dances until an hour after they started. Beth smiled when she saw how the girls clustered together around a balloon arch, while the boys seemed magnetically drawn to the punch table. Music was playing, but no one was dancing yet.

Beth glanced down. Brooke, not Kimmy or Michelle, had helped her pick out a blue satin floor-length dress that Brooke had worn to her junior prom. With her dad still out of work, Beth didn't even think about asking to buy a new dress. The only jewelry she wore was the locket Jake had given her.

She hadn't really talked to Jake all week, but he had asked her Thursday in the hall if she was still going to the dance, so she figured things were fine. It was funny, she thought, that he hadn't offered her a ride. It felt strange walking into the room alone.

She didn't see Jake anywhere, but Reed's friends Gina and Jackie spotted her and waved her over. Relieved, Beth crossed the empty dance floor to where the girls stood.

"You guys look great," Beth said, examining Gina's black floor-length dress with a blue sash that matched the blue streaks in her hair. Jackie's black dress had pink insets, and she wore pink poodle earrings. Kimmy and Michelle would not approve, but Beth loved it.

"You look really glamorous," Gina said to Beth. "We dressed up just for fun."

"Don't kid yourselves. You two look awesome!" Beth assured them. "Have you seen any of the guys around? I haven't seen Reed or Jake anywhere."

Gina and Jackie exchanged glances but didn't say anything. Just then, the gym doors opened again and in walked Jake, flanked by Nick, Scottie, Michelle, Kimmy, and a pretty seventh grader named Heather. Most of them were laughing and kidding around, but Jake and Heather hung back, whispering to each other. Beth was slightly annoyed that Jake wasn't scanning the room for *her*.

When Beth finally caught Jake's eye, he looked at her and smiled. But it wasn't a pleasant smile. Beth didn't understand what was going on. She crossed the room, and as she approached Jake, his friends grew quiet.

"I thought you'd never get here," Beth said, trying to sound confident. "Do you want to dance?"

"Absolutely," he said. Then he reached for Heather's hand to lead her onto the dance floor.

Beth was afraid she might throw up, but just as she felt her stomach lurch, she heard Reed say, "She wasn't talking to you, board brain. She was talking to me."

Reed, who was standing right behind Jake and Heather, walked between them and held out his hand to Beth. She took it gratefully, and he pulled her onto the dance floor.

The music, which had been fast, ended, and the DJ played a slow song. Glad as she was to be rescued, she felt a little embarrassed about a slow dance with Reed. She stood there, awkwardly, until he took her hands and placed them on his shoulders. Then he rested his hands lightly on her waist. Beth caught a glimpse of Jake over Reed's shoulder and almost laughed at the look on his face.

"Thank you," Beth whispered.

"I am but a humble knight," Reed said, bowing his head, "charged with rescuing young maidens from evil lords. But I find my work immensely satisfying."

Beth laughed, but as she did, tears came to her eyes. "I've been such an idiot, Reed. You were right about Jake all along."

"Hey there," he said, brushing a tear off her cheek, "don't let him see you cry. Besides, knights don't carry tissues."

Beth took a deep breath and smiled. Then she looked at Reed. She'd never seen him in a suit before. He looked good—really good. He smelled nice too. Suddenly, she felt even more awkward about dancing so close to him.

"By the way," Reed said to her, "you look beautiful tonight. Promise me you'll still dance with me at our senior prom."

"Of course," she said. "And thanks for trying to cheer me up."

"Humble knights just speak the truth," he said, looking at her until she broke his gaze.

They danced in silence for the rest of the song. Beth realized she'd just been dumped by Jake, and she didn't even really care.

"After the dance, could I ask some advice?" Reed asked.

"Of course," she replied. "I owe you one."

"You always say that," he said.

"It's always true," she replied.

The song ended, and the DJ switched to faster

music. Soon Jackie, Gina, Ian, and some other guys from the anime group joined them on the floor. When the next slow number started, Ian asked Beth to dance with him. She said yes, but spent most of the time looking over Ian's shoulder, watching Reed dance with Jackie.

After a while, Beth was wiped out. She'd been training so hard with Ty all week that she didn't have much energy for dancing. So she and Reed got some punch and headed for a table far enough away from the speakers that they could hear each other.

"So what advice do you need?" Beth asked when they were seated.

Reed looked a little embarrassed. "Well," he began, "there's a girl I really like, but I don't know how to tell her."

"So what advice do you need?" Beth asked. "You can talk to anyone."

"I just don't want to blow it. We're pretty good friends, and I don't want to make her feel weird about me."

Beth's mind was racing. Was it Jackie? Gina? For some reason, she didn't like the idea at all. But Reed had been so great to her that night. She knew she had to help him.

"Can I just tell you what I would want to have happen, if it were me?" Beth said.

"OK," Reed said. "Sure."

"Most girls don't need you to do anything extravagant or crazy," she began slowly.

"You mean, like flowers and things?" Reed asked.

"Flowers are OK, I guess," Beth said. "Maybe just one flower—like a rose."

"Rose," Reed repeated, as if memorizing it. "Got it. What then?"

He was making her nervous. What did *she* know? "OK, maybe not a rose. Maybe that's too much."

"OK," he repeated again. "No rose."

"Oh, Reed, for Pete's sake, I don't know. If it were me . . . ," she began and then paused.

"If it were you . . . ," he said.

"If it were me, I'd want you, I mean, someone, to talk to me casually—not make it some big deal. I'd get too nervous. I'd like him to just tell me that he was glad we were really good friends, but he was wondering if it could be a little more."

"So no skywriting or fireworks or carriage rides?"

"Nope. Just someplace casual, public, relaxed, and with a group. Be honest, but don't put a lot of pressure on her to answer right away."

"So, I'm confused. Rose or no rose?"

She laughed. "Look, I'm really no expert. Let's just say you have a rose somewhere nearby to give her in case things go well."

"Sounds like a plan," Reed said.

At ten-thirty, Beth said good-bye to everyone, and Reed walked her out to wait for her mom. Beth told him about Ty's crazy training for the Open.

"I don't know," Beth said to Reed. "Is this what I'm supposed to be doing with my life? Snowboarding?"

"You really don't have to decide right now, Beth," Reed said. "There are lots of things I want to do. I love art and anime, but I'd also like to get better at guitar so that maybe I could start a praise band. Maybe even become a youth minister."

"Wow," Beth said. "I'm impressed. I still don't know what I want to do on Monday."

"But you know what you want to do Sunday, don't you?"

"Make Jake eat snow?" Beth said.

"Exactly!"

Reed reached around Beth's neck and unclasped the locket Jake had given her and placed it in her hand.

"You look better without this," Reed said.

"I feel better without it too," she replied.

Just then Jake and Heather came walking out, holding hands. Beth tossed the locket at him. He clumsily fumbled to catch the piece of jewelry before it hit the ground.

"There, now you can give her something meaningful too," Beth said sweetly. "Just take my picture out of it first."

Heather glared at Beth and then at Jake. They both walked away, and Beth laughed. "That felt good."

"Oh, he doesn't have a chance at the Open," Reed said confidently.

Mrs. Summers pulled up. "Do you need a ride home, Reed?" she asked.

"No thanks," he said. "My mom will be here in a minute."

As they pulled away, Beth's mom said, "That Reed is so nice—much nicer than the Bahlman boy."

Beth couldn't agree more.

CHAPTER:09

Ty and Beth worked together all day Saturday, using the *DDR* game and the hula hoop. Beth wondered why she was doing it instead of spending the day at the slopes. But Ty was her coach now, and as she had learned from Brooke, you do what the coach tells you to do.

"So why are we dancing, Ty?" Beth finally asked.

"Are you challenging my authority?" he said with mock irritation.

"No, just curious what your plan is," Beth said.

"Your body needs to be really flexible," Ty said. "And you need to use your whole body when you're competing. You get really stiff when you jump and spin. If you'd relax and turn your hips, your spins would improve. Thus, the hula hoop."

"Makes total sense," she said.

"Beth," Ty said, "you're good enough to win without this kind of training. But if you keep working at it, you've got what it takes to have a shot at the Olympics in a couple of years."

"Really?" Beth asked.

"Absolutely," Ty said. "And if I'm still here then, I want to be the guy who coaches you."

She arrived home that night, exhausted and nervous. *I'll never be able to go to sleep*, she thought. When she went to the kitchen for a glass of milk, she found her dad sitting at the kitchen table.

She hadn't really talked to him since the afternoon he told her he'd lost his job. Did he even know about the Open? She wasn't sure, but she realized she should have talked to him about it days before.

"Do you have a minute, Daddy?" she said. She bit her lip.

"Sure, Beth," he said, sounding tired. "What is it?"

"I just wanted to tell you, I'm competing in the Teen Open snowboarding competition tomorrow."

"I know," he said. "I also know," he continued, "that you almost chose *not* to compete."

"Yeah," she said. He sounded angry. This wasn't going well. "Daddy, I'm sorry to disappoint you. I just couldn't stand the thought of not competing."

"I'm disappointed in you," he said, "but not for the reason you think. When Brooke told me—yes, Brooke told me—that you'd let some kids at school persuade you not to go out for the Open, I was really surprised."

"It wasn't just them," Beth said, feeling like it was time to be totally honest. "It was you too."

"I know. Brooke told me." He looked down at his hands for a moment and then said, "Beth, I've been wrong about you. I always thought you'd taken up snowboarding because it was cool, because your friends did it, and most of all as some way to hurt me."

"Daddy!" Beth said. How could he think she snowboarded to *hurt* him?

"Let me finish. I thought I was upset because you didn't want to be a competitor. But I realize now that it was because snowboarding took you away from me. As a skier, I could help you—coach you. As a snowboarder, I'm no good to you."

Tears welled up in Beth's eyes, but she didn't cry. "You were still my dad. You *are* still my dad."

Her dad reached over and placed his hand on top of hers. "When I heard that your friends actually were encouraging you *not* to compete, and you had, even for a few days, considered doing what they wanted, I realized how proud I was of you for deciding to stand up and be yourself. Whether you were standing on skis—or a snowboard," he said.

"So," Beth asked, hardly able to believe what was happening, "are you coming tomorrow?"

"You bet. I'll be the one cheering the loudest."

It felt weird. For so long she'd fought against him. She didn't know how to just relax and be with him.

"Thanks, Daddy," she said and kissed him on the head. She started to walk out of the kitchen.

"Beth?" he said. "I'm—"

"I know, Daddy," she said. Her heart was so full already. She didn't even need to hear him say "sorry."

As she lay in bed, she thanked God for what had just happened. "I knew you used to do miracles in the Bible," she prayed. "I just didn't know they still happened."

The next morning, when her alarm went off, Beth knew she was as ready as she could be. She hopped out of bed and got to the shower before Brooke.

Beth smelled oatmeal cooking as she came down the stairs and into the kitchen. Her mom was at the stove, and her dad was reading the paper. Beth was relieved to see that it wasn't the classifieds. She thought he needed a break from job hunting. She leaned over and kissed him on the cheek.

"Morning, Daddy," she said.

"Morning to you too, sweet pea," he said with a grin. "Ready for today?"

"Yep!" she said. "Look out, mountain, here I come." It felt good to hear her dad laugh again.

The phone rang, and when she answered, it was Reed.

"Just wanted you to know I'll be thinking of you. I might not make it out of church in time to see the beginning of the competition, but I'll be there as soon as I can. Think your folks can save me a seat?"

"Sure," she said. "Say a prayer for me at church. And tell everybody I'll *definitely* be at youth group next week."

Beth hung up the phone and sat at the table. It was great to hear Reed's voice, but it made her nervous. She kept thinking about their conversation at the dance and wondering who the girl was.

Her father interrupted her thoughts. "Reed's not the only one who will pray this morning," her dad said. "I'd like to say a blessing too." Beth was surprised, but bowed her head as her father began. "Gracious and loving God, thank you for my family. Thank you for my wife and two daughters. Today, Lord, I ask that you please watch over Beth and keep her safe. Help her to do her best in the competition. Remind her that she's a champion. Thank you for this food, which gives us strength. And thank you for my job interview tomorrow. Amen."

Beth thought it would be rude to burst in on her father's prayer. But as soon as he finished, she said, "What?"

"Actually, it's a second interview," he said. "I think I've got a really good shot."

"Dad, that's fantastic," she said.

"Thanks," he answered. "But today is your day. I'm so proud of you."

A few minutes later, Ty showed up. "You ready, squirt?" Ty asked.

"I even *dreamed* about hula-hooping last night," Beth said.

"Good," Ty said. "When we get to the registration, they'll give us a course map for the race and also tell us which run you'll do your downhill on."

"There are two races?" Beth's mom asked.

"Yes, ma'am," Ty said, "an obstacle course for time and a freestyle run for points."

"Do you think there's a chance it'll be in the Serpent's Mogul with the half-pipe?" Beth asked.

"It could be," Ty said. "But I have a feeling that, for your age bracket, it'll be something like the Cyclops. It's wider, and there are only two platforms with room to navigate around. They may save the Serpent's Mogul for an older bracket."

"Are you familiar with the Cyclops?" Beth's dad asked her.

"Yep," she said. "I've ridden every course there is on the mountain!"

"Well, if we don't see you until after the race, just know we love you," her dad said.

"And don't worry," Brooke whispered as they left

together. "I'll capture it all on the video camera."

Beth had a hard time sitting still and felt like she could hardly breathe. Now that everyone—including her dad—was so excited for her, so confident that she would win, she felt really nervous. After all, Jake wasn't such a bad boarder. Especially, she thought wryly, after all she had taught him. And she didn't even know what the other competitors would be like.

Later, Ty, Brooke, and Beth sat at a table inside the Avalanche Grill, studying the course sheet they had been handed at check-in. Beth was slated to be the first to run the obstacle course. First, though, she'd have to make it through a time trial, which neither of them thought would be a problem, and then compete among the final six. The judges had chosen, just as Ty had suspected, the Cyclops and Lower Cyclops runs for the course. The runs were full of divots and moguls to make the race interesting.

Brooke attached a white square with a large, red, block number 6 to the front and the back of Beth's pink bib jacket. Beth looked down at the number. It was official. And she was officially a nervous wreck.

At ten o'clock, a horn blew signaling the beginning of the time trials. The trials were at Dante's Cutoff, a short but difficult run. The chairlift took all of the competitors to the top of the mountain, and one by one, they were to drop into the Cauldron. The objective was to get their bearings as they went through the Cauldron so that the clock would start running at the point where the Cauldron and Dante's Cutoff intersected. Twenty competitors in the young teen category all stood in line for their turns. Beth saw Jake once, but didn't say anything to him. He ignored her completely.

The line judge blasted one whistle blow, signaling the next racer to start. The time trials would go quickly, with a two-minute interval between each snowboarder. Beth stood at the line and snapped her boots into the bindings.

"Hey, number 6," an official called, "put on your helmet!"

Startled, Beth quickly strapped on her helmet and positioned herself at the beginning of the run.

It would take her just about two minutes to get through the Cauldron and to the starting line of Dante's Cutoff. The whistle blew, and she dropped into the course. The Cauldron was a narrow trail that led to a 180-degree curve before ending at Dante's Cutoff.

Beth concentrated hard. This run was not about jumps or fancy stunts. The sole purpose was to post a qualifying time. But the speed was determined on the Cutoff, not here in the Cauldron. She needed to get used to the feel of the newly made snow beneath her feet and maneuver through the bumpy terrain carefully so that she was calm and sure when she completed the curve and moved forward into the straightaway of Dante's Cutoff.

Beth eased around the corner and saw an official—still at least fifty yards ahead of her—standing at a starting line, preparing to start his clock. She leaned into the board and squatted down to cut the wind resistance. She could feel the wind against her body and hear it whipping by her helmet. She maintained her position as she crossed the starting line and propelled herself down the straightaway. She could already see the finish line ahead of her, but there was a surprise. A course had been roped off. She would have to navigate through it. At the right time, just as the slope began to level off, she extended her legs, still keeping them bent at the knee, and eased her way through the course, swaying her hips back and forth, just as Ty had instructed.

"Twenty-eight and 33/100ths," the official called out.

"Is that a good time?" Beth asked.

"I think it'll hold up," Ty said. "Let's go wait inside for the announcements. I want to keep your muscles as warm as possible before the race."

Beth posted the fastest qualifying time. Jake was fourth. Two other guys took the second- and third-place positions. To Beth's delight, another girl placed fifth. Another guy placed sixth. The six finalists were led to the racing course. Jake stayed clear of Beth, who made an effort to talk to the other girl who would be competing. The girl's name was Amanda Albright, and she had come up from Alpine Valley in southern Wisconsin.

"Are you related to Brooke Summers?" Amanda asked.

"She's my sister," Beth said.

"She was my counselor last summer at church camp. She was so awesome."

"Yeah, she's pretty special," Beth said.

"I saw a write-up on her in a magazine last month."

"Well," Beth said, not knowing what else to say, "good luck."

"Thanks, Beth," Amanda replied. "You too."

The two girls took their positions. Beth's time put her in the lead position on the inside of the course. Luckily, Jake was far away from her. Beth snapped her boots back into her bindings and prepared for the run. She paused and closed her eyes, thanking God for all that had happened that weekend.

Please keep us all safe, she prayed silently. Then she added, *Even Jake.*

The official called for the competitors to get ready. Beth rolled her shoulders to stay relaxed. The official raised his pistol into the air, and the gun sounded.

Beth dropped into the run instantly. Ty had told her never to look side to side to see if anyone was close by. He told her to worry only about the course. Within fifty feet of the starting line was a jump. All of the boarders had to jump, and it narrowed, so there could be collisions. But Beth stayed ahead of the others and cleared the jump, rocketing out and gaining a good fifteen feet of air before landing. She saw no one near as she approached the first series of cones.

She eased into the course and swiveled her way through it, coming out onto a straightaway that led to another jump at the top of Lower Cyclops. Beth took the jump and leaned into it as she flew over a crowd of spectators. She curled up into a ball, grabbing the bottom of her board to stabilize herself.

As the ground approached, she eased up and touched down at the foot of a series of moguls. She thought about going around and weaving through them, but this was not the time for that. She needed to stay focused on the finish line, which lay in front of her just one hundred yards away.

With one jump to go, the path narrowed, and Beth spied a board to her left just over her shoulder. She was pretty sure it was Jake. She bent into the board again and pushed with her body. She reached the platform ahead of him. She sailed over the jump and arched before touching ground right before the finish line. Beth was amazed by the cheers she heard as she won the race. The crowd was chanting, "Summers, Summers," just as she'd heard so many times before for Brooke. But now they were cheering for *her*.

She removed her helmet to catch her breath and look around. Her mom and dad, Brooke, and Reed were there, and so were Gina, Jackie, Otto, Joe, and Ian. She noticed that a girl from Reed's debate team named Tricia stood near Reed. *Is she the one he likes so much?* Beth wondered.

The announcer called for attention. "In third place, number 14, Jake Bahlman. In second place, number 4, Marc Wang. In first place, ladies and gentlemen, number 6, Merrimac, Wisconsin's own Brooke, I mean, *Beth* Summers."

The crowd again cheered as Ty ran up to Beth and raised her hand into the air. "Come over here," he said. "Brock and Blake want your autograph."

A few moments later, the announcer explained that the officials needed to clear the obstacles for the freestyle competition. The six competitors were led into the heated trailer to warm up. Ty stayed outside with Brooke and her family. From inside, Beth looked out the window at the crowd. Her eyes kept being drawn to Reed and Tricia.

Beth tried to make herself be happy for Reed.

It didn't help that she was now sharing the trailer with Jake, along with the other competitors. He still was treating her as if she were invisible. He looked a little shaken, actually. If Amanda hadn't fallen before the finish line, Jake would not have placed at all.

I wonder what he thinks of me, Beth thought. He'd manipulated her, she knew, and gone out of his way to hurt her at the dance. But she couldn't help thinking that she'd hurt him too. After all, *she* was the one who said she wouldn't compete and then changed her mind. She tried to put herself in his position. Maybe he wasn't totally to blame. She whispered a prayer, "Help me, God!" and walked over to where Jake was sitting, flipping through a magazine.

"You must be awfully happy with yourself," he said. "Are you just *trying* to humiliate me?"

Beth almost mentioned how he had tried to humiliate *her* at the dance. But she didn't want to go down that road. "I just came to say I'm sorry."

"Sorry for what?" he asked.

"Sorry that I wasn't honest with you or myself. I should never have told you that I wouldn't compete. I can understand why you got mad."

Jake shrugged. "Whatever. You obviously just weren't the kind of girl I was looking for."

"Yeah," Beth said. "I tried to be, but I wasn't. Anyway, good luck."

"Uh-huh," Jake said, and went back to reading his magazine.

Even though Jake had been a jerk about it, Beth felt better after she talked to him. She knew she'd done the right thing. Now she just had to focus on the second half of the competition.

As winner of the first round, Beth was given the option and chose to go last on the freestyle. She wanted to rest and focus. As she stood at the top of the Cyclops run, she stretched, and jogged in place to stay warm. The Cyclops had two jumps within one hundred feet of each other. In her mind, she played out her course of action.

Watching on a portable monitor, she saw the crowd cheering as Jake did his freestyle run. He had jumped in the air and completed a full 360-degree spin before touching ground. Beth regretted ever teaching him the move. But she had to admit he did it pretty well. The way the points broke down, he was still very much in the running. But she was determined to win.

The official shot his pistol into the air, signaling for Beth to begin. She had noticed how the boys seemed to jump into the slope, but Beth gently dropped into it, using that hula-hoop motion in her middle to gracefully move back and forth. She made herself relax and breathe in as she began building speed down the Cyclops. Beth crouched into the jump and spread her arms wide. The smile beneath her helmet was visible only to God, but Beth knew he had seen it. Touching down, she again slowed herself by weaving in and out of the moguls in her path before coming into the straightaway leading to the two jumps.

Beth approached the jump with peace and confidence. As she projected off the platform and straightened up her body, she twisted herself from the hips and went into a spin, completing a solid 450-degree turn. She landed backwards and her board shot forward, down the stretch and into the next jump. Airborne again, Beth executed another perfect 450-degree, setting her down in the right direction. When she crossed the finish line, she knew, whatever happened, she couldn't have done any better.

"A 9.1 is great," Beth's dad told her after the scores were announced, "considering the next boarder under you scored an 8.1. You could have gotten another two-tenths of a point if you'd—"

He stopped when he saw the look on Beth's face. "It doesn't matter. You were fantastic," he said.

"Thanks," Beth said. "Thanks, Dad."

CHAPTER:10

El Diablo's was crowded for a Sunday night. Beth, Ty, and Brooke sat in a corner booth talking about the day and watching the snow falling heavily outside.

"I'm serious," Ty said for the fifth time. "Beth, you were fantastic. I wouldn't be surprised if you won a gold medal before you turn eighteen."

"Right now I just hope we get *dinner* before I'm eighteen," she said. "I'm starving."

Beth quickly looked up as the front door opened. She hoped Reed would stop by to celebrate with her, but instead she saw Jake walking over to their table.

"Hey," Jake said. "Congratulations. You did awesome."

Given how their last conversation had ended, Jake's changed attitude was a big shock.

"Thanks," Beth said uncertainly.

"Could I talk to you for a minute?" Jake asked.

"I guess," Beth said, scooting out of the booth to go

talk in another corner. "So what did you want to say?"

"Well, um," Jake said nervously, "I just wanted to apologize for being such a jerk. That was really cool, what you said in the trailer this afternoon. I just wasn't in the mood to hear it." He reached into his coat pocket and pulled out the locket.

"I bought this for you, and I want you to keep it," Jake said, handing it to her. As he did, the front door opened again. This time it was Reed, with Ian, Jackie, and Tricia. Reed instantly spotted Beth and started walking over to her. When he saw Jake, he paused.

"Keep it, Jake. Really," she said, anxious to get away from him. What would Reed think? "But thanks. That took guts. And by the way, you really are a great snowboarder."

"I had a great teacher," he said, and went over to where his friends were sitting.

Beth headed straight for Reed. "I thought you'd never get here!" she said.

"Tricia's mom invited us back to her house for dinner," he said. "But we all wanted to get some hot chocolate. And besides, I wanted to see you. There's something I need to talk to you about."

Beth glanced over her shoulder and saw something that made her stomach knot up. Tricia was holding a rose.

"I really need to get back to Brooke and Ty," she

said, suddenly eager to run away. She didn't want her perfect day spoiled by hearing Reed tell her about Tricia.

"It'll just take a minute," Reed said, looking uncomfortable.

"Fine," she said. "What's up?"

"One question first. Is this casual enough?" Reed asked.

She thought he was talking about his clothes. He was wearing his normal long-sleeved T-shirt and jeans. What did he mean?

"Sure, I guess," she replied.

"No fireworks or skywriting anywhere around, right?"

She began to wonder if Reed was going crazy. "No," she said, "not that I can see."

"Great," he said. "Then there's something I need to say to you."

For a moment, Beth was confused. It almost sounded like *she* was the girl Reed wanted to talk to. But she put that thought out of her mind. She was quite sure he would never think of her in that way.

She stood there, staring at the ground, waiting to hear his next words, but he didn't say anything for a moment. She finally mustered the courage to look up at him. He was staring at her in a funny kind of way.

"What?" she said.

"Uh, you know, we've been friends for a long time," he said nervously.

"Best friends."

"Right, best friends," Reed said, shuffling his feet.

"Reed, just spit it out. You've asked Tricia to be your girlfriend." It hurt Beth to say it.

"What?" He looked confused. "No! I mean, she's great, but—"

"But what?"

"But I want you to be my girlfriend," Reed blurted out.

Beth's eyes lit up. "Really?"

"Yeah," he said, looking relieved he'd finally said it. "I know I'm just some geeky comic book collector and anime freak you hang out with, but—"

"Me too," she said, interrupting him.

"You too, what?"

"I mean, I want to be your girlfriend too."

Reed looked at her, smiling. "Wait right here," he said. "I've got something for you."

He went to the table where Tricia was sitting and brought back the rose. "I brought this for you, but I made Tricia carry it in. I didn't really think I'd get a chance to give it to you."

Beth laughed, remembering their conversation at the dance. "I saw it when you came in, but I thought the rose was *for* Tricia."

Reed told her how Tricia was Ian's girlfriend and that she was even excited to get to know Beth better. "Come and sit with us," he said. "That is, if Brooke and Ty don't mind."

"I'll go check," Beth said, "but I'm sure they won't." She started to walk away, and he grabbed her hand.

"Beth," he said, "you look pretty cool tonight."

She glanced down at her jeans and sweater. With the events of the day, she hadn't even had a chance to put on a drop of lip gloss, and she knew she had helmet-head hair. It felt great to know that she could just be herself with Reed. Without thinking, she leaned in and kissed him on the cheek.

"What was that for?" he said, smiling.

"Now," she said, "you owe *me* one."

Then she ran to ask Ty and Brooke if they would mind if she sat with Reed and his friends. They didn't.

As she crossed the restaurant to Reed's table, she thought about what Brooke and Mrs. Nagle had said. She thought about her dad, Jake, the Open, and Reed.

God really *had* worked everything together for good, even though Beth didn't always feel like she was all that close to God. But after everything that had happened lately, Beth was pretty sure she wanted to get to know God better—much better!